A
PROSECUTOR
FOR THE
DEFENSE

David Brunelle Legal Thriller #4

STEPHEN PENNER

ISBN-13: 978-0615914671
ISBN-10: 0615914675

A Prosecutor for the Defense

This is a work of fiction. Any similarity with real persons or events is purely coincidental. Persons, events, and locations are either the product of the author's imagination, or used fictitiously.

Joy Lorton, Editor.
Cover by Nathan Wampler Book Design.

THE DAVID BRUNELLE LEGAL THRILLERS

Presumption of Innocence

Tribal Court

By Reason of Insanity

A Prosecutor for the Defense

Substantial Risk

Corpus Delicti

Accomplice Liability

A Lack of Motive

Missing Witness

Diminished Capacity

Devil's Plea Bargain

Homicide in Berlin

Premeditated Intent

Alibi Defense

Defense of Others

Necessity

A PROSECUTOR
FOR THE DEFENSE

A person who is not a member of the State Bar of California but who is eligible to practice before the bar of any United States court, and who has been retained to appear in a particular cause pending in a court of this state, may in the discretion of such court be permitted to appear as counsel pro hac vice, *provided that an active member of the State Bar of California is associated as attorney of record.*

California Rule of Court 9.40

CHAPTER 1

King County homicide prosecutor David Brunelle sat at his computer, trying to read the police reports for his latest case directly off the screen. His boss, Matt Duncan, had decided the office needed to move toward 'paperless' prosecution. Lawyers without paper were like birds without wings, but Brunelle knew who his boss was, and more importantly, he respected him. So he agreed to do his part. He would read the reports off the screen for as long as he could stand. But when trial time came, he was printing them out and putting them in a damn binder.

"David!"

Brunelle was jarred by the sudden appearance of Kat Anderson in his doorway. She was the best assistant medical examiner in the county. She was also his girlfriend.

"Kat." He stood up and started around his desk for her. "What are you doing here?"

She wasn't one to drop in unannounced. He always got a call or a text before she stopped by his office. Hell, she did that before she stopped by his apartment for the night. So he thought something might be wrong. When he got next to her, he was sure of it.

Her eyes were glistening at the corners. Kat Anderson didn't cry. Not in front of him anyway. It was, selfishly he knew, one of the things he liked about her. No drama. But looking down at her just then, the tears welling in her eyes, his heart felt sick.

"What is it?" he asked. "What's wrong?"

"I need your help, David," she said. Her voice broke just a little. Not much though. She was a strong woman.

"Help with what?"

"Promise me," she avoided the question. "Promise you'll help me."

"With what?" he repeated.

"Promise me," she insisted.

So he did. "Of course. Whatever it is, I promise."

She finally exhaled. She closed her eyes and wiped them, then nodded and looked up at Brunelle. "Thank you."

She stepped around him into his office. He trailed behind.

"So what did I just promise to do?" he asked.

She nodded and turned around. "It's Jeremy."

Brunelle felt his expression harden. 'Jeremy' was Kat's ex-husband. They didn't say his name a lot. He was usually referred to as 'Lizzy's dad.' He lived in California with his second wife. Or maybe it was his third. Brunelle knew he was a doctor too—a plastic surgeon, of course. And that was about all he wanted to know about him.

But apparently, there was more.

"What about him?" he asked.

"He's in trouble."

"What kind of trouble?" Brunelle was getting tired of the vagaries. He'd just promised to help his girlfriend's ex-husband somehow. He was already irritated by that. The guessing games weren't helping. "Come on, tell me what's going on."

Kat took a deep sigh, then sat down on the edge of Brunelle's desk. "Jeremy's been arrested."

"Arrested?" Brunelle tried to give a concerned expression, devoid of the jealous joy he got out of the information. "For what?"

Kat shook her head. "Murder."

Okay, now that wasn't funny. "Murder?" he repeated.

"His wife was found murdered in her dance studio," Kat explained. "He got arrested yesterday." She stood up and grabbed Brunelle's suit coat. "But he's innocent, David. He didn't do it. He can be a complete asshole, but he's not a killer."

Brunelle nodded. He understood Kat's emotions, if only because he'd dealt with a lot of distraught family over the years. The victim's family was often in denial about the loss of their loved one, but the killer's family was usually in denial too—about what their family member was capable of. That Nile was a pretty big river.

"Okay," he said noncommittally. "You want me to call down to the California prosecutor and see what's going on?"

Kat gave a half-smile and shook her head. "No, David. I want you to be his lawyer."

Brunelle's eyebrows shot up. "His lawyer? I can't be his lawyer. I'm a prosecutor."

"Only in Washington," Kat pointed out. "You're not a prosecutor in California."

"I'm not even a lawyer in California," Brunelle retorted. "I'm only licensed in Washington."

"But you can get a limited admission for a particular case, can't you?" Kat asked. "I've seen that before. Sometimes we get lawyers from other states who get a 'pro hack' admission or something to deal with the legal issues around what to do with the body."

"It's *pro hac vice*," Brunelle corrected. "And yes, I suppose that's possible. I mean, I'd have to ask the California bar for special permission."

"They'll give it to you."

"And get time off from Matt."

"He'll do it."

"I don't know their court system," Brunelle continued to protest. "Their evidence rules are totally different."

"You'll figure it out. You'll learn it. You can do it, David. You know you can."

Brunelle sighed. "Kat, this is crazy. I can't do this."

"It's Lizzy's dad," she reminded him.

He shook his head, "Kat…"

She grabbed his chin and locked eyes with him. "You promised."

He stared into her eyes. She was smart to have come to his office. He couldn't look her in the eye and say no.

"Okay," he relented. "I'll do it."

CHAPTER 2

Brunelle frowned and looked at the clock. 9:17. He'd stalled long enough. He could only refresh his email so many times. He pushed himself up from his desk and walked the short distance to his boss' office.

Duncan's secretary, Tammy, had just brewed a fresh pot of coffee and was starting one of the thousand tasks she had every morning as the administrative assistant to the elected District Attorney. She was tall, pretty, with long brown curls and a bright smile. And she was good as hell at her job. She was also the sentry to Duncan's office.

"Is Matt available?" Brunelle asked, hands in his pockets.

"He's on the phone," Tammy answered, looking at the indicator light on her own phone. "Oh, wait. He just hung up. Go on in."

Brunelle stepped around Tammy's desk and into Duncan's large corner office, with its panoramic view of Elliott Bay and the Olympic Mountains beyond. "Hey, Matt. Got a minute?"

Duncan turned from where he was checking his own email and stood up. "Of course, Dave." He gestured toward his conference table and came around his desk to join Brunelle. Duncan usually avoided the 'Boss Behind the Desk' dynamic when he could. At least with Brunelle. "What's up?" he asked.

Brunelle grimaced and rubbed the back of his neck. "Um, well," he struggled to explain, hardly believing it himself. "Do you know Dr. Anderson at the medical examiner's office?"

Duncan grinned. "You mean your girlfriend? Yeah, I've heard of her."

Brunelle could feel a blush despite his 40-plus years. He was still unaccustomed to having a 'girlfriend' and even less so having everyone know about it. He surrendered a small, nervous laugh. "Yeah, her. Um, she kinda needs my help with something."

"Okay," Duncan replied casually. "Why wouldn't we help the M.E.'s office? We're all on the same team."

Duncan didn't get it. But then, why should he? Brunelle hadn't explained it yet. So he did. At least as much as he knew himself. Kat's ex-husband lived in San Francisco. He was remarried. His new wife was murdered. He'd been charged with the crime. Kat asked him to be his attorney. He'd said yes.

Duncan listened intently. Finding out about other people's problems was always interesting. When Brunelle finished, he nodded for several seconds. "Wow," Duncan finally said. "You're whipped."

Brunelle threw his hands up. "Wow," he echoed. "Not really the reaction I was looking for."

Duncan laughed. "You're a career prosecutor, but you're going to play defense attorney to your girlfriend's ex-husband a thousand miles away. And you're surprised anyone calls you whipped?"

Brunelle shrugged, no reply at the ready. He wasn't really surprised anyone thought it. He just hoped people might not say it.

Duncan's smile softened. "Must be love."

Brunelle shrugged again, even less ready with a reply.

Duncan saved him. "So..." His smile twisted into a serious

expression. "Are you quitting?"

Brunelle's eyebrows shot up. "No!" he practically shouted. "God, no. No, this is just a one-time favor. I'm not quitting. I just need a leave of absence."

Duncan exhaled. Brunelle hadn't even noticed he'd been holding his breath. "Whew. Good," Duncan said. "I don't want to lose you." He thought for a moment. "You know we can't pay you during a leave of absence, right? Especially if you're doing defense work."

Brunelle nodded. "I know. I've got some money saved up. I'll be okay."

"How long do you think it'll take?" Duncan asked.

Brunelle shrugged. "Not sure. Just a couple of months, I hope. It'll be my only case, so I can push it to trial pretty quickly."

"Do you think that's smart?" Duncan questioned, already switching back from friend to trial attorney. "For your client, I mean. What's his name again?"

Brunelle grimaced. "Jeremy." He hated saying the name out loud. "And yeah, it's smart. If they're anything like us, they won't expect a murder case to go to trial for at least a year. If I just refuse to waive speedy trial, I can force them to trial before they're really ready. Waiving speedy trial is usually stupid, I think. A rushed prosecution is a sloppy prosecution, and that'll be good for me. After all, it's their burden to prove everything beyond a reasonable doubt."

Duncan laughed. "*Our* burden," he corrected amicably.

Brunelle surrendered a laugh too. "Right, that's what I meant."

Duncan tapped his chin for a moment, then stood up and went to his desk. He pulled open one of his desk drawers. "I'm going to give you the name of a guy I knew in law school. Andy Dombrowski. He ended up becoming a defense attorney and moved to San Francisco." Duncan stepped around again and handed Brunelle a well-worn business card. "Look him up when you get there. He's a good guy. He'll give you some pointers."

"Thanks, Matt." Brunelle took the card and put it in his shirt pocket.

Duncan sat down again. "So what are we going to do with your cases for three months while you're off playing Perry Mason?"

Brunelle nodded. He'd already thought about that too. "I think I can resolve a couple of them. The rest I'll set over 'til I get back."

"What if they won't waive speedy trial?" Duncan teased.

Brunelle grinned. "They will. Just because I'm smart doesn't mean they are."

Duncan smiled. "We'll see. But even if they do, I don't want those cases just sitting there. I want someone to watch over them, just in case something comes up."

Brunelle frowned, but nodded. He didn't like handing his files off to someone else, but Duncan was right. Things come up. Detectives got new leads; witnesses got scared; newspaper reporters asked questions. "What about Fletcher?" he suggested. "Or Wilson? They're both reliable."

But Duncan shook his head. "No, I was thinking about Michelle Yamata."

"Oh," Brunelle managed to reply at the thought of the attractive young prosecutor.

"You tried a case with her, didn't you?" Duncan asked. "You said she did a good job."

"She did a great job," Brunelle replied. "Exquisite."

"Okay then." Duncan patted the table. "It's settled. I'd like to see what she can do."

Brunelle nodded and smiled. "Me too."

* * *

"Wow," Yamata said after Brunelle called her up to his office and explained the situation. "You're whipped."

Brunelle was speechless for a moment. He just stared at her.

She shrugged. "Just sayin'."

"Yeah, well," Brunelle stammered, "maybe it will make me a better prosecutor."

"Maybe," Yamata said and leaned back in her chair opposite Brunelle's desk, "but good luck as a boyfriend."

Brunelle cocked his head. "What does that mean?"

"It means," Yamata absently twisted her silky black hair into a loose ponytail, "she's got you dropping everything and jumping through hoops like a trained poodle. What are you gonna do if you win and ex-hubby is out on the street again? That joyous reunion is going to involve a lot of hugs and kisses—but you're going to be watching it all from across the courtroom."

Brunelle frowned. That hadn't occurred to him. "I don't think so," he asserted.

"Well, no worries." Yamata shrugged and leaned forward, tossing her hair back over her shoulder. "You're in control."

Brunelle's brow creased. "How do you mean?"

Yamata laughed darkly. "You can always throw the case. Nothing too obvious, just make sure he gets convicted. Then you get your Kitty Kat all to yourself."

CHAPTER 3

Brunelle slipped off his belt and looked Kat in the eye. "This is my favorite part."

Kat bent over. "Behave, David," she said as she slipped off her shoes. "Unless you want a full body cavity search."

Brunelle glanced around the security checkpoint at Seattle's Sea-Tac International Airport. If he did want such a search, it probably wouldn't be right there, right then. But it probably would have involved Kat. He pulled off his shoes and put them in a plastic bin along with his belt, cell phone, and keys. He slid the bin onto the x-ray machine's conveyer belt. "Well, you're the expert on body cavities."

Kat smiled. "Most of the bodies I see have a few extra cavities." She slid her own plastic bin onto the conveyer belt. "Besides," she leaned against him and purred, "you seem to know your way around some body cavities."

Brunelle felt his heart race and his blood rush. He peered down at the beautiful woman looking up at him. He wrapped his arm around her waist. "Remind me again why we're flying and not taking a long, romantic drive down the coast with lots of stops at local hotels."

"Ugh. Stop it you two." Kat's teenage daughter Lizzy walked up and dropped her laptop bag into a bin. She pulled out her earbuds and put her iPod in the tray as well. "We're in public."

Kat looked sideways at her daughter, then planted a big kiss right on Brunelle's lips. "Sorry, honey," she laughed. "We'll try to behave."

Brunelle wouldn't have been very interested in behaving just then, but the presence of Kat's daughter, a half dozen scowling security officers wearing rubber gloves, and the ten million travelers in line behind him returned his focus from his girlfriend to the metal detector he needed to walk through.

One of the gloved security officers pointed at him. "Next!"

He turned back to Kat, wiggling his toes in his socks. "I hate feeling like a criminal."

Kat had to laugh. "Said the man who puts people in prison."

He shrugged and fought off a frown. *And now tries to get them out again.*

* * *

Their flight departed from Gate N7. They had to take the underground tram from the main terminal to the north satellite. Once there, they took the escalator up and walked down the concourse to the gate. Lizzy trailed slightly behind, listening to her music, glancing around, and generally lost in her own thoughts.

"She seems okay," Brunelle observed quietly to Kat.

Kat shook her head. "It's an act. She's scared to death."

Brunelle stole a glance at Lizzy, then turned back to Kat. "What about you?"

"Me?" she said. "I'm angry."

"Angry?" Brunelle repeated. "Really? Why is that?"

The scowl that had seized Kat's face couldn't quite hold on. "Don't get me wrong," she said. "I'm worried too. I'm not that big of a bitch. We were together a long time. We have a child together. I consider him a friend. But this is just confirmation that he's the same self-centered prick he was when we were married."

"Jeremy Anderson, Prick," Brunelle joked. "Maybe that's how I'll introduce him to the jury."

Kat cocked her head, then laughed out loud. But it wasn't really that funny. Brunelle said so.

"It's not that," she said. "It's hearing you say 'Jeremy Anderson.' His name is Stephenson, not Anderson. Oh my God, he'd be so mad if you called him Jeremy Anderson."

"Stephenson?" Brunelle asked. "Not Anderson? Did you go back to your maiden name after the divorce or something?"

Kat shook her head. "No, I never took his name. I wasn't going to be Kat Stephenson."

Brunelle considered. "I dunno. It has a certain ring to it."

Kat grimaced. "Yeah. A real Peace Train, Cat's in the Cradle kind of ring. No, thank you."

Brunelle had to laugh. "Oh yeah. Okay. I can see that." Then he asked, "You didn't want to hyphenate? Kat Anderson-Stephenson?"

"Nope," Kat replied. "Anderson Stephenson sounds like an accounting firm. And too many syllables anyway."

Brunelle nodded. "Yeah, that is a lot of syllables."

"Five's my limit," Kat explained.

"Five?" Brunelle cocked his head. "Why five?"

Kat rolled her eyes. "Think about it, Romeo. Let me know when you figure it out."

Brunelle did think about it. Then he figured it out. Then he blushed and changed the subject. "Well, anyway, maybe this time it's not his fault."

"Maybe." Kat shrugged. "I don't really care."

"You don't care if he's guilty or not?"

"Well, of course," Kat admitted. "I want him to be innocent. I don't want him to be a murderer."

They'd arrived at N7. Lizzy marched forward and plopped into a seat in the boarding area, pulling her phone out as she did so to text or tweet or whatever it was kids did any more. Brunelle and Kat lingered in the walkway.

"What I really care about," Kat pointed at her daughter, "is her. Being a teenage girl is hard enough as it is. She doesn't need the stigma of having a father in prison. She's worked really hard—hell, I've worked really hard—to get us where we're at. But do you think she's going to keep friends once they find out her dad's in prison? Even if the friends understand, what about their parents? Would you let your daughter hang out with a girl whose dad's in prison for murder?"

Brunelle looked over at Lizzy. That was a lot to think about all of a sudden. Kat took his hand.

"So thank you for doing this," she said. "I know you're doing this for me. But don't do it for me." She nodded toward Lizzy. "Do it for her."

CHAPTER 4

The first stop was the hotel. It was in San Francisco's Fisherman's Wharf area, rather than downtown. In addition to being a little cheaper, it was also a nicer place for Kat and Lizzy to hang out while Brunelle was away working on the case. In addition, it was just barely within walking distance of the Haight-Ashbury neighborhood, famous for its bohemian counter culture, and home to the office of attorney Andy Dombrowski. Dressed in a full suit, Brunelle felt a little conspicuous as he reached the neighborhood. He figured that must be why Dombrowski chose to put his office there. Why else would he be so far away from the courthouses downtown except to make visiting prosecutors from other states uncomfortable when they came begging for help?

Upon meeting the gentleman, however, it became clear that Andy Dombrowski was in his element. The office was located on the second floor of two-story building, above a used clothing boutique and some sort of restaurant or bar or spa or club or something. Brunelle wasn't quite sure. The windows were darkened but peering inside, the business appeared to deal more with making people feel a certain way than with providing them with objects. He found it both disconcerting and appealing. Like the light in front of an angler fish's jaws. He decided there would be time later to explore mysterious clubs in strange parts of town. He had business to attend to.

Kat and Lizzy had stayed back near the hotel to explore the beach and shops and restaurants, so when Brunelle reached the small lobby of Dombrowski's office he allowed himself to be taken in by the beauty of the very young receptionist Dombrowski was fortunate to employ.

She had long, curly brown hair, piled haphazardly in what he and his college buddies used to call the 'just fucked' look. Heavy eye make up, lots of earrings and rings, and tattoos covering most of her visible skin up to her jaw all served to accentuate rather than distract from her naturally breathtaking bone structure and general fitness. "Hello," she greeted him in a high, almost squeaky voice. "Can I help you?"

Oh, I'm sure you could, Brunelle thought, but he was smart enough to say instead, "Is Mr. Dombrowski available?"

"Do you have an appointment?" the receptionist asked.

Brunelle shook his head. "I'm afraid not. I was referred by a friend."

The young lady smiled. "Well, that's good to hear. Andy's in his office. He always makes time for new business."

Brunelle cocked his head at the receptionist as she stood up and stepped toward the closed door of the only office in their suite. "New business?" he asked.

"Right," she replied. "New business. You want to hire Andy, right? He always makes time for new clients."

Brunelle finally understood. He was about to explain that he was not in fact a criminal defendant looking for a lawyer, when the young lady with too much make up and too many tattoos cocked her own head and looked at him appraisingly. "Sex crime?" she guessed.

"What?" He was flabbergasted. "No," he protested. "No, I'm not charged with a sex crime."

The woman raised her hands defensively. "Oh, sorry. It's just, with the suit, trying to look all respectable, and the way you were ogling me when you came in, well, I just figured you were some kind of pervert."

"I'm an attorney," he protested.

"Oh, right," she choked back a laugh. "No attorneys are perverts." She shook her head and giggled. "But it explains the suit. I'll get Andy."

She knocked on the door and slipped inside while Brunelle fought off his indignation at being mistaken for a sex offender. He replayed the conversation in his mind and had just realized that he'd forgotten to insist he wasn't ogling her when the office door opened again and Andy Dombrowski stepped out to shake his hand.

He was a large man, a little taller than Brunelle and a lot heavier. He had long gray hair, thinning in the front and pulled into a ponytail in the back. His plastic rimmed glasses slid down his nose from the oil that generally glistened on his features. He had at least one day's worth of salt-and-pepper stubble, and yellowing teeth that were on full display when he smiled broadly to greet his visitor. "Hello there! Kylie tells me you're a lawyer. You're not in some kind of trouble, are you? Kylie says you're not a pervert."

"I said he's not charged with a sex crime," Kylie corrected and she gave Brunelle a wink. He watched in stunned admiration as she retook her place at the reception desk.

"What can I do for you, good sir?" Dombrowski effused.

Brunelle finally pulled his eyes away from Kylie and looked at Dombrowski. "Matt Duncan sent me. I need some help."

* * *

"Wow." Dombrowski leaned back in his chair when Brunelle had finished explaining. "You're—"

"Don't say 'whipped,'" Brunelle interrupted.

Dombrowski stared at him for a second, then burst out

laughing, falling forward in his chair and almost choking he laughed so hard. "Ha ha ha. No. No, I was going to say, 'Wow, you're fucked.' But yeah, maybe that other thing too."

Brunelle decided not to protest the 'other thing.' Instead he inquired about the 'you're fucked' thing. "Why am I fucked?"

Dombrowski managed to stop laughing. In part because he was done; in part because of what he started thinking about in order to explain his 'you're fucked' comment. "Have you met the prosecutor yet?"

Brunelle shook his head. "No. I came here first. I need a local attorney to sponsor me. Matt said you'd do it."

Dombrowski nodded. "Oh, I will. But it won't help you any."

Brunelle wasn't sure what that meant. "Why not? Do they not like you or something?" He could definitely think of some defense attorneys he didn't like. Then again, he could think of some prosecutors he didn't like either.

"No, they don't like me at all," Dombrowski replied with obvious pride. "I don't play their games. They're dirty, the whole lot of them. And I call 'em on it."

"Dirty?" Brunelle replied. He knew what Dombrowski was alleging; he just had trouble believing it.

"Yup," Dombrowski replied. "The elected D.A. is Tom Kincaid. Wants to be governor someday. Best way to do that is to make sure everybody knows your name. Best way to do that is to be in front of the cameras as much as possible. Best way to do that is to charge sexy cases, no matter how weak the evidence is or how innocent the defendant is."

Ah, thought Brunelle. Dombrowski was a 'true believer.' All prosecutors were dirty. All defense attorneys were heroes. All defendants were innocent.

He nodded and said, "Oh," in a way that he thought would suggest he believed Dombrowski. Apparently not.

Dombrowski laughed, but it was mirthless. "It's okay. Don't believe me. But you'll see." He leaned onto his desk and folded his thick hands in front of him. "Let me ask you this: is your girlfriend's ex innocent?"

That, Brunelle realized, *was one hell of a good question*. "I don't know."

Dombrowski shook his head. "Well, you better figure it out, Dave," he said. "But guess what?"

"What?"

"Even if he is innocent. Even if you can *prove* he's innocent, you're fucked. Kincaid never dismisses cases."

Brunelle shrugged. "I don't dismiss too many cases either."

"You're not getting it, Dave," Dombrowski pressed. "You know your client is innocent. Your girlfriend wouldn't have asked you to defend him if he wasn't."

Brunelle wasn't so sure of that.

"But it doesn't matter," Dombrowski went on. "They don't care. Kincaid has a murder case and he's going to get a murder conviction, evidence and ethics be damned."

Brunelle was beginning to bristle at the attack on his particular branch of the profession. "Just because a prosecutor pursues a case vigorously doesn't make him dirty."

"It does if the defendant is innocent."

"Well, that doesn't happen very often," Brunelle replied. "It's not supposed to anyway."

Dombrowski grinned sardonically and leaned back in his chair again. "How many innocent people are in prison right now, Dave?"

Brunelle shrugged. "I don't know."

Dombrowski nodded. "Exactly. You don't know. But do you know what your answer should have been? It should have been, 'zero.' There shouldn't be any innocent people in prison, but there are. And it's because of prosecutors like Kincaid. Like that guy in

North Carolina who went after the lacrosse players. Like the guy who put that football player away for five years for a rape he didn't commit. Don't even get me started on the death penalty."

Dombrowski shook his head, a deep frown creasing his thick features. "I remember Matt. He was a good guy. It sounds like, talking to you, he still is. But Kincaid isn't. And you're fucked."

Brunelle exhaled deeply and tried to take in what Dombrowski was saying with both an open mind and a grain of salt.

"You're one of us now, Dave," Dombrowski said, "For your client's sake—and your girlfriend's—you better start thinking like it."

CHAPTER 5

The San Francisco County Courthouse was actually called the 'Hall of Justice.' Like the Superfriends' headquarters. Brunelle had always liked the Superfriends. But with Dombrowski's words still echoing in his head, he actually wondered whether he was going to like the prosecutors whose offices—along with the San Francisco P.D., the county medical examiner, and even the county jail—were housed inside the famous art deco structure that filled an entire city block. He even let himself wonder whether these prosecutors were actually seeking justice, at least for his client.

He'd known overzealous prosecutors before. Every office, every organization, has its jerks. His office was no exception. Neither was the public defender's office or the bench. But it was easier to tolerate an intransigent, 'no deals' prosecutor when he was on the same side of the table as you.

Brunelle stepped through the front doors and queued up for another pass through the metal detectors. He could see this trip was going to involve a lot of humiliation and body cavities. To that end, he refastened his belt and walked over to the elevators, steeling himself for the reception he fully expected from the San Francisco D.A.'s office.

The receptionist for the prosecutor looked a bit different from the one employed by Dombrowski. She was probably just as young, but her hair was straight and shoulder-length, she had no visible tattoos, and her make-up was barely noticeable. She also wore a conservative dark suit and a minimum of appropriately shiny jewelry.

"Hello," she greeted Brunelle as he entered the lobby. "Can I help you?"

Despite his current role, he felt far more comfortable than he had in Haight-Ashbury. "Yes. I was wondering if I could talk to the prosecutor assigned to the Jeremy Stephenson murder case."

She smiled as if she knew which case he was talking about— she might or she might not, there were a lot of cases in San Francisco—and then asked the obvious question.

"And how are you related to the case?"

The answer would direct her response. If he were the detective, he'd likely get full access to the prosecutor. If he were family of the victim, he'd at least get a Victim Advocate to come out to the lobby to see what his questions were. If he were a reporter, he'd probably get the run-around. And the defense attorney? He'd probably get some shit.

"Actually, I'm a prosecutor from Seattle." When that succeeded in raising the young woman's eyebrows, he followed up, ambiguously, "It's a long story."

Both of those statements were true, even if entirely misleading when joined together in that order in response to that question. He almost enjoyed it.

"Oh, okay," said the receptionist. "Just a moment, sir. What's your name?"

"Dave Brunelle. Thanks." Then he quickly took a seat in one of the faux-leather chairs in the waiting room.

A few minutes later, a young man in a dark suit with short brown hair and fashionable glasses opened the door and greeted him.

"Mr. Brunelle? I'm Jim Westerly. I'm the prosecutor on the Stephenson case. You're here all the way from Seattle? I didn't know there was any Seattle connection."

Brunelle stood up and shook Westerly's hand. "Oh, there's a Seattle connection, all right. You got a few minutes?"

Westerly grinned, realizing something was going on. "Sure," he said anyway. "Come on back."

* * *

"So, wait," Westerly interrupted half way through Brunelle's explanation. "You're going to be Stephenson's defense attorney?"

Brunelle shrugged. "I'm afraid so."

Westerly ran a hand through his fine brown hair. "Wow."

Don't say I'm whipped, Brunelle thought.

He didn't. Instead, he nodded and stuck out an appraising lower lip. "Okay. Well, great. Maybe that's a good thing. You'll get where we're coming from on this. Excuse my French, but your guy's fucked. Have you talked to him yet?"

Brunelle shook his head. "No. First stop was my local associated counsel. Then here. I'll talk to him next."

Westerly offered a cautious grin. "Who's your local counsel?"

Brunelle could guess this wouldn't help gain any trust, so he tempered it with an explanation. "My boss, the elected D.A. up in Seattle, knew a guy in law school. Andy Dombrowski."

"Dombrowski?" Westerly half laughed, half spat. "That guy? Oh my. Well, you're in for one hell of a ride, Mr. Brunelle. Did he tell you we're all dirty?"

Brunelle had to laugh. "Yeah. Although he didn't mention you by name."

"Who did he name?"

"Kincaid. And everybody who works for him."

"Yeah, well that's everybody here." Westerly replied, still amused at the thought of the defense attorney. "Listen, I get that you need to have local counsel to appear here, but keep your distance from him if you can. He's a little loopy, if you ask me. Obviously, we're not dirty. No more than you guys in Seattle are. But I guess you gotta tell yourself something every morning if you make your living helping the worst society has to offer."

Brunelle nodded. He'd kind of always thought that too when dealing with the true believers. "Don't worry," Brunelle assured. "He agreed to sponsor me, but we're not about to form a partnership or anything."

"Good," Westerly answered. "Just stay as far away from him as you can, and you'll be all right. So what do you know about the case?"

Brunelle frowned slightly and shook his head. "Not much. I know it's a murder case. I know he's accused of murdering his wife. And I know his ex-wife is my girlfriend. After that, I'm kinda in the dark."

"Well, here's the sixty-second version," Westerly offered. "Stephenson and his missus—who's a good ten years younger than him, and an aerobics instructor to boot—were having pretty serious financial difficulties. Then suddenly, her aerobics studio burns to the ground and she's found dead inside. At first it looks like an accident, like she just died of smoke inhalation. But then the autopsy shows no sign of smoke in her lungs. So the medical examiner looks a little more closely and sure enough there are fingerprint bruises on her neck. Stephenson strangled her to death, then set the fire to cover his tracks. And when the detectives go to ask him some questions, he lawyers up. So here we are."

Brunelle nodded. It didn't sound like that strong of a case. No confessions and no eye witnesses. Then again, motive, means, and opportunity usually meant guilty as charged.

"You said you haven't talked to your guy yet?" Westerly asked.

"Right." Brunelle nodded. "I wanted to talk to you first."

"Well, it's probably a good thing you did," Westerly answered. "I'll get you copies of the police reports so you can read them before you talk to him. Then when he tells you his story, you can call bullshit on him. Or not. Your choice. But at least you'll know when he's lying to you. Because there's one thing you can be sure of."

"What's that?" Brunelle asked.

Westerly smiled. "They always lie to their lawyers."

Brunelle sighed, but smiled back. "I know."

CHAPTER 6

The jail was on the other side of the Hall of Justice. Brunelle thought they might have been called holding cells on the cartoon. Or something cheesy like Justice-Cells or Science-Cells. He wasn't sure. But either way, Jeremy Stephenson was in a cell, and Brunelle was going to visit him.

It was a bit exciting to actually get to talk to a defendant directly. As a prosecutor he was prohibited from ever talking directly to a defendant. He always had to go through the defense attorney. Even when he got those voicemails from the lady at the state mental hospital who wanted to talk about a plea bargain because her assigned lawyer was too stupid to understand that she was guilty, he still had to go through her lawyer.

But the rush wore off when his client stepped into the consultation booth and Brunelle saw through the glass partition just how bad and just how good Jeremy Stephenson looked.

He was dressed in ill-fitting orange jail jammies. His skin was gaunt and yellowy after only a few weeks out of the sun. His cheeks were a bit sunken, suggesting he didn't like the food on the inside. And his expression couldn't quite hide the panic he must have been feeling at the prospect of spending the rest of his life in prison.

On the other hand, Jeremy Stephenson was one hell of a

handsome man. He looked to be an inch or so taller than Brunelle, with thick brown hair that had just enough wave to be interesting without being unruly. Large biceps stuck out of the jammies and a well-developed chest pushed against the orange fabric. His features were chiseled and he had that chin that no one had except Superman and the ex-husband of your new girlfriend.

He sat down opposite Brunelle. There was no phone like in the movies; they could hear each other through a round metal grate embedded in the plexiglass. A small slit at the bottom was just big enough to slide papers through in case a signature was needed for court.

"Mr. Stephenson," Brunelle started. "I'm David Brunelle. I'm going to be your lawyer."

Jeremy nodded, a smile tugging at the corner of his mouth but entirely failing to reach his eyes. "Call me Jeremy. And thank you, Mr. Brunelle. Kat says you're the best."

"Call me Dave," Brunelle replied, "And Kat's full of shit."

That caught Jeremy's attention. That smile reached his eyes after all. No doubt he'd thought the same thing many times over the years.

"I'm not a defense attorney, Jeremy," Brunelle explained. "I've never been one and I don't ever want to be one. Not even now. I'm doing this because Kat asked me to. There are undoubtedly better attorneys for this. I don't know California law. I don't know the local procedures. I don't know the local judges. I'm not the best prosecutor there is, so I'm definitely not the best defense attorney there is. But I promise you I will do everything I can to get you acquitted and back out on the street again."

Jeremy stared at Brunelle for a several seconds, processing what he'd said. Finally, he asked, "Why?"

"I told you." Brunelle nodded. "Kat asked me to."

And that same look of understanding sparked in Jeremy's eye.

No doubt he'd done things for her for the same wholly inadequate and completely sufficient reason. "Okay," he said. "That's good enough for me."

Brunelle smiled. They understood each other.

"Tell me everything," he said.

Jeremy shrugged. "I don't know what to tell you. My wife is dead. I'm in jail. I don't know any more than that."

"I'm sure you know a lot more than that," Brunelle replied. Actually, he was glad for Jeremy's answer. It seemed like the kind of thing a truly innocent man might say. He didn't start with his alibi or a justification. He started with not knowing what the hell was going on. "Let's start with your wife. Tell me about her."

Again, Brunelle got a reaction he liked. Jeremy started to cry. Not that fake cry he'd seen defendants try to pull off in court, big on high-pitched sobs and low on tears. This was just the opposite. No noise, but eyes glistening and a tensing of the jaw as he fought off a quavering lip.

"Vanessa was the best thing that ever happened to me," Jeremy said. Then he raised a finger. "No, the best thing that ever happened to me was Lizzy. And maybe Kat for giving me Lizzy. But that's complicated. But after Kat and I split up, well, I was in a bad place and Vanessa rescued me from it."

"A blond California aerobics instructor ten years your junior," Brunelle pointed out. It had to be said. Westerly was sure as hell going to say it as many times as possible during the trial.

Jeremy grinned and looked down. He suddenly looked every bit as old as Brunelle, despite the muscles and the tan. "Yeah, I know. Actually, she taught dance. And she was fifteen years younger. That probably just makes it even worse."

Brunelle shrugged. "Probably. But it's also understandable. It doesn't mean you killed her. Maybe just the opposite. Did you have a pre-nup?"

Jeremy shook his head. "No. I didn't care about that. I was doing well with my practice, but nothing spectacular. She didn't marry me for the money. And by the end, there wasn't any anyway."

"That's what I heard," Brunelle confirmed. When Jeremy looked askance at him, he explained, "I already met with the prosecutor."

"Ah," Jeremy nodded. "Of course you did. Old dog, new tricks, right? Well, then you know that we were pretty much tapped out."

"Is that why she was going to leave you?" Brunelle tried to pull a detective trick. It didn't work.

"She wasn't going to leave me, Dave," Jeremy replied. "But nice try. Are you sure you're on my side?"

Brunelle nodded. "I'm sure. I just wanted to see what you'd say. Not all clients tell their lawyers the truth. One of the true joys of my job is pointing out to defense attorneys during plea bargaining how their clients totally lied to them. I don't want that happening to me. Everything you tell me is confidential. I won't tell anyone—not even Kat. I don't want to sound harsh, but you're not worth losing my license over, so if you tell me something, I'm not going to risk my career by violating the attorney-client privilege. So you might as well tell me the truth. The truth usually comes out anyway. I'd rather not be surprised when it does."

Jeremy nodded for a few seconds. "The truth, huh?"

Brunelle nodded back.

"Okay," Jeremy looked down again. "The truth is, I think she was cheating on me."

Fuck, thought Brunelle. "That's a pretty classic motive for murder."

"I know," Jeremy replied, looking back up. "Why do you think I didn't talk to the cops? I wasn't going to lie to them, but I couldn't tell them the truth either."

"Any idea who she was cheating with?"

Jeremy sighed. A deep, pained, fully betrayed sigh. "My business partner, Gary Overstreet. He did her breast augmentation. I think it started after that."

Of course it did. Welcome to Cali, Mr. Brunelle.

He didn't want to overwhelm Jeremy on their first meeting, but he did need to know at least one thing before he left. "Where were you the night Vanessa died?"

Jeremy shrugged. "I was home."

Brunelle frowned. "Was anyone with you?"

Jeremy raised an indignant eyebrow. "No," he protested a bit too loudly.

Brunelle waved away the suggestion. "I didn't mean it that way. I was just hoping you might have a witness to verify your alibi."

"Oh," Jeremy relaxed a bit.

"There are other ways to confirm that stuff," Brunelle said. "Did you do anything online? Maybe we can get a search history or something to show someone was using the computer that night."

Jeremy thought for a moment. "No. I watched some TV then went to bed early and read until I fell asleep."

Brunelle frowned. "Kindle?" Maybe they could get some records for that somehow.

Jeremy shook his head. "No. Just a regular old-fashioned book. Paper and ink."

"Well, that's no help at all," Brunelle replied.

He tapped the counter and frowned. He decided he didn't feel like discovering more unhelpful information just then. There was really only one more question he needed an answer to.

"Did you kill your wife, Jeremy?"

Jeremy looked Brunelle straight in the eye. "No, sir."

Brunelle nodded. *Yep*, he thought. *They always lie to their lawyers.*

CHAPTER 7

After dinner at one of the seafood joints on the Fisherman's Wharf strip, Brunelle, Kat, and Lizzy went for a walk along the beach. Eventually, Lizzy strayed off toward the lapping waves and Brunelle could finally bring up the one thing they hadn't talked about during the meal—which was ridiculous, given that it was the reason they had all traveled a thousand miles down the coast.

"Jeremy looks like he's holding up okay."

Kat let out a large exhale that Brunelle didn't even know she was holding in. She squeezed his hand. "Good. That's good to hear."

He smiled slightly and looked down at her. "All things considered," he added.

She laughed slightly. "Yeah."

"Sorry you couldn't come today," he went on. "Visiting hours are tomorrow, but the lawyer can visit any time."

"No worries," she answered. "I think Lizzy needed a day to get ready anyway. No one wants to see their dad behind bars."

"Well, technically, he's behind glass," Brunelle corrected. "But yeah."

Kat squeezed his hand and looked up at him. "Thanks for being exact," she teased.

He grinned. "It's another one of my charms."

"Uh-huh," she replied dubiously. "So, what did he have to say?"

Brunelle cocked his head. "What?"

"What did he say?" Kat repeated. "About the case?"

"I can't tell you that," Brunelle gasped, half-laughing at the very question.

Kat pulled up short, still holding his hand. "What do you mean you can't tell me?"

"Attorney-client privilege," Brunelle answered. He resisted the urge to add, 'duh.'

Kat thought for a moment. "Well, I think *I'm* your client. I'm the one paying you."

Brunelle smiled and pulled her back into a walk. "First of all, you're not paying me anything. I'm doing this *pro bono*, remember? Second, it wouldn't matter if you did. If some kid gets in trouble and his parents hire a lawyer, the kid's still the client. The lawyer can't tell the parents anything the kid doesn't want them to know."

"Well, Jeremy's not my kid," Kat replied. "He's my ex."

"Exactly. If I couldn't tell a paying parent what their kid told me, how could I possibly tell a non-paying ex-wife?"

Kat stopped them short again. "So, wait a minute. You're telling me that my ex-husband could have confessed to the entire murder to you and you wouldn't tell me?"

Brunelle drew a pretend zipper across his lips. "Attorney-client privilege."

He could see the irritation in Kat's eyes. But he could see something more. Something that hurt his heart.

"He didn't confess to anything, Kat," he said. "He said he didn't do it."

He watched the flicker of fear in her eyes die out and she started walking again. She laid her head against his arm. "Thanks,

David."

He didn't say anything. Jeremy wasn't worth violating his ethical duties, but apparently Kat was. And apparently, he was okay with that.

"So he's looking okay?" she asked. Lizzy had taken off her shoes and was ankles deep in the water.

"Oh yeah," Brunelle replied. "He's a good looking guy, even after being inside for a bit."

"A good looking guy?" Kat repeated with a chuckle. "My goodness, Mr. Brunelle, do I detect a hint of jealousy?"

Brunelle surrendered a nervous laugh. "Not at all, madam. I'm just making an observation. He's a good looking man. He obviously takes pride in his appearance, and it shows."

"Yep," Kat laughed. "Jealous."

"Now why would I be jealous?" Brunelle asked. "He's in jail and I'm walking along the beach with a beautiful woman and her delightful daughter."

"How about because that particular delightful daughter is his, and the reason she exists is because of things he did with that particular beautiful woman?"

Brunelle forced a nod. "Thanks for helping me think of that. I hadn't quite gotten the visual down."

Kat laughed. "Oh, please. Like you've never been with anyone else."

"That's not what I said. I said, I wasn't jealous."

Kat was silent for a few moments. "You're lying, aren't you?"

Brunelle shrugged but didn't reply.

She hugged his arm and laid her head against it again. "Thanks."

"For helping your murderous ex-husband who fathered your child?"

"No," she replied softly. "For being jealous."

CHAPTER 8

A week later found Kat and Lizzy ready to head back north and Brunelle ready to head into the lion's den for the first pre-trial conference. As much as Kat wanted to stay for the whole case, there was no way she could miss work for three months. And even if she could have, Lizzy couldn't be out of school that long. But it wasn't all bad news. The night before had been memorable, with Lizzy in her adjoining suite behind the closable door. And now he could focus on his case with minimal interruptions. He transferred from the expensive tourist hotel on the water, to an extended stay hotel halfway between downtown and whatever the worst neighborhood in San Francisco was named. It didn't matter; it was close to the courthouse. Or rather, the Hall of Justice.

Pretrials were pretrials, whether in Seattle or San Francisco. The building was different, the courtroom was different, the lawyers and the statute numbers were different, but the basic purpose was the same: defense attorneys trying to get a deal. Brunelle found the courtroom for the pretrial on People v. Stephenson and walked into the adjoining conference room. Just like in Seattle, the room was full of prosecutors and defense attorneys, wheeling and dealing between jokes and showing off kid pictures and telling stories about what they did that weekend. The only difference for Brunelle was that, up north he knew everyone. And down south, he was a defense attorney.

He spied Westerly sitting at a table against the far wall, talking with a woman who was obviously a lawyer, but not obviously on one side or the other. He walked over and interrupted their light banter.

"Hey, Jim," he said. "Dave Brunelle. I'm not sure if you remember, but I'm handling the Stephenson murder case."

'Handling.' He still couldn't quite bring himself to say 'defending.'

"Oh, right. Hi, Dave," Westerly replied. He pointed toward the woman he was speaking with. She reminded Brunelle a bit of Jessica Edwards, one of the public defenders he routinely went up against back home. This woman also had straight blond hair, a dark suit, and minimal make up. So for some reason Brunelle was surprised to hear she was a prosecutor. "This is Natalie Halvorson. She's in our drug unit. I was just telling her about our case."

"Oh yeah?"

"Yeah," Halvorson answered. "Are you really representing this guy because your girlfriend asked you to?"

Brunelle sighed inside, but kept a pleasant smile plastered to his face. "Something like that. It's kind of complicated."

"Seems kind of simple," Halvorson replied. Then she made a whip-cracking noise and gesture.

"It's a bit more than that," Brunelle insisted. He didn't like the recurrent ribbing, but he liked even less that he was on the outside of the prosecutors' club. He liked least of all that he had to take it if he wanted Westerly to offer his client a deal. "But that's okay. I'm hoping maybe we can settle this case and I can get back to Seattle and put on my white hat again."

Westerly rubbed his chin. "Yeah, I don't know, Dave. Your guy murdered his wife. I'm not sure what kind of deal I can give." He opened his file absently, as if there were some secret documents inside that would tell him exactly what offer to make. And as if he hadn't already considered it and decided what the offer would be. If he had, it was important that Brunelle talk to him. If he hadn't, it was even more important.

Having been reminded of Jessica Edwards, Brunelle tried his best to emulate her. He couldn't replicate the hair toss, but she'd let it slip once that there were three things she always told the prosecutor during negotiations. First, her guy wasn't a bad guy; he just made a mistake. Second, it was never going to happen again; he'd taken steps—drug treatment, anger management, whatever—to help him not re-offend. Those two were important because prosecutors were scared to death of cutting a deal to the wrong guy. They didn't want to end up on the front page because some guy they gave a deal to ended up shooting kids in a park or running over grandma in a crosswalk.

The third thing was the tricky one. She pointed out the weaknesses in the prosecutor's case. Gently, fairly, but unequivocally. Prosecutors, you see, were spoiled. They usually won their trials. They were supposed to win. They weren't supposed to prosecute innocent people, and they had entire police departments doing all their investigation for them, Throw in twelve jurors who don't want to live in a country where innocent people are prosecuted, and the defendant had almost no chance of an acquittal. So losing stung. Defense attorneys were used to it. Prosecutors were scared to death of it. So show them where their case was weak. Make them sweat a little bit. Make them scared of coming back up to the office and having to tell everyone that the jury acquitted. And do that right after you've told them what a great guy your client is and how he'll never, ever do it again. Really. Pinky promise.

Thankfully, Halvorson excused herself, and Brunelle went into his pitch. "Look, Jim. I know this seems like a bad case, but let me tell you a little bit more. Maybe some stuff you don't know. First off,

Stephenson isn't that bad a guy. He's got no criminal history at all. He's a professional. And he's got a great daughter living up in Seattle, who loves the ballet. You like the ballet?"

Westerly grinned and crossed his arms. "No," he said, leaning back in his chair. "Sorry."

Brunelle kept his smile pasted on. "No worries. The point is, he's never done anything like this before, and he's not likely ever to do it again. He's a doctor, a father, a husband—"

"Ah, see," Westerly interrupted. "That's the issue. He's not a husband. Not anymore. Because he killed his wife. And I'm not too worried about him doing it again, because he's never getting out again."

Hmm, Brunelle frowned. *This must be what it's like for Jessica.* Well, she would have pressed forward, so he did too. Parts one and two were only going to go so far in a murder case. Time to move to part three.

"Well, that's the thing," Brunelle said. "He only never gets out again if you convict him as charged. Premeditated murder. But your case isn't as iron-clad as you made it sound when we first met. I've reviewed the reports. There are holes."

Westerly's smile faded. Brunelle hoped that, although he was doing the defense attorney shtick, he might have more credibility given his normal job.

"What kind of holes?" Westerly asked.

Okay, good. I've got his attention.

"Well, for one thing, the case is completely circumstantial," Brunelle started. "He didn't confess and you have no eye witnesses. You're piecing it together based on who the most likely suspect is."

Westerly shrugged. "Plenty of cases are circumstantial."

"Sure they are," Brunelle agreed, "and a jury will convict on circumstantial evidence if it's no big deal. If it's a burglary and the defendant is arrested a few blocks away with the stolen TV. Okay.

Fine. They know he'll get some jail time, but not the biggest crime in the world. But this is a murder case. Even if we don't tell them what sentence my guy is looking at, they'll know it's a lot. Hell, some of them might think it's a death penalty case, and you and I both know the case law doesn't let the judge tell them it's not. So there they are, twelve jurors, faced with the biggest decision anyone could have, and you're going to tell them my guy did it because, hey, usually the husband does it and he never said he didn't."

Westerly had to laugh. "You know I can't tell them he lawyered up."

"Even better for me," Brunelle replied. "Your coroner will say she died before the fire. Great. So somebody choked her out, but how do you know it was my guy? It could have been anybody. A burglar, an angry client, a lover."

Westerly's eyebrows shot up. "A lover? You're going to say she was having an affair and her lover killed her?"

Brunelle smiled. He was kind of liking this defense attorney gig. "It doesn't matter what I say. I don't have to say anything. You have the burden of proof. Can you prove, beyond a reasonable doubt, that she *didn't* have a lover, that she *wasn't* killed by that lover?"

Westerly pressed his fingertips together and tapped the index fingers against his lips. Finally a smile unfurled across his face. "I'll tell you what. I'm not buying your jilted lover story, but you have a point about your guy having no history and likely never doing anything like this again. I'll offer a Murder Two and Arson One. He pleads to both of those, he'll be eligible for parole after twenty-five years."

Brunelle suppressed his own smile. Jessica's little spiel had worked. At least in part. Brunelle knew Westerly had most likely walked in that morning willing to make the Murder Two offer, but that didn't mean he was just going to do it. Sometimes you just don't make deals—at least not until the defense attorney points out the weaknesses in your case. And Brunelle thought it was a pretty fair offer. Probably exactly what he would have offered.

"I'll talk to my client," Brunelle said.

"Good," Westerly replied. "The offer's open for one week. If he turns it down, then we're going to trial on the Murder One and he can die in prison."

"Understood," Brunelle answered. Then he smiled. "I'll see what I can do. I can be pretty persuasive sometimes."

CHAPTER 9

"No. Fuck no. No fucking way." Jeremy pounded a fist on the shelf of the consultation room. "I'm not pleading guilty to murder. I'm not pleading guilty to anything. I didn't do anything!"

Well, fuck, thought Brunelle. This wasn't going to go well after all.

"It's a fair offer," Brunelle said. "Probably what I would have offered."

"Well, fuck you too, then." Jeremy was furious. "You're not a prosecutor any more, Brunelle. Not on this case. You're a defense lawyer. You're *my* defense lawyer. So get it through your thick head: I'm innocent. I didn't do anything. And I'm not pleading guilty to anything."

Brunelle frowned and leaned back in his chair.

"Understood?" Jeremy pressed.

Brunelle didn't like being pressed. He grinned and leaned forward. "Understood. Perfectly. No deals. Fine. It's not my ass that's looking at life in prison. But I understand where you're coming from. I've been doing this a while. I throw around numbers like 'twenty-five years' as if they don't mean anything to anyone. But I hear you. You're innocent. Good. That makes my job easier. But there are plenty of innocent people in prison, Jeremy. So if this doesn't work out, and you do get life, I want you to remember this offer and that is was you, not me, that turned it down."

"Fine." Jeremy waved an angry hand at him. "I'll remember."

There was an uncomfortable silence for several seconds as each man got lost in his own thoughts. Finally, Jeremy said, "Do you believe me?"

"About what?" Brunelle asked.

"About being innocent. Do you believe I'm innocent?"

Brunelle thought for a few moments, holding his chin in his hand. He sighed. "Yeah, I do. Not that it matters. You could tell me you were guilty and exactly how you did it, and I'll still do my job. But yes, damn it, I believe you."

Jeremy visibly relaxed in his chair. Then he smiled. "Why 'damn it'?"

"Because there would be a lot less stress if you were guilty," Brunelle admitted. "Sitting next a man who might go to prison for the rest of his life is bad enough. Sitting next to an innocent man who might go to prison for the rest of his life? Now, that's stress."

"I can think of something more stressful," Jeremy said.

"Oh yeah? What?"

"Being that innocent man."

Brunelle nodded. "Yeah, I guess you're right."

They sat in silence for a few more moments. Then Brunelle sat up a bit straighter and leaned onto his own little shelf. "I'm going to have to do some research. I'm going to talk to people and ask questions. If you're right about your partner, that's something I'm going to have to pursue, even if it's embarrassing. I'm going to make some people uncomfortable, maybe even mad. That's probably a good thing, but I need to know, before I go wading into that, I need to know the truth. About everything."

Jeremy nodded. "Okay."

"So, I believe you when you say you're innocent," Brunelle repeated. "But is there anything else I should know? Anything you've kept secret or hidden that impacts this case in any way? Because I don't want to be surprised by anything."

Jeremy looked down and thought for several long moments. Finally, he looked up again. "No. There's nothing else."

"Are you sure?"

"I'm sure."

And so was Brunelle. Of two things. Jeremy Stephenson was in fact innocent. And he was still lying.

CHAPTER 10

"I don't know, Kat," Brunelle said into his cell phone that night as he sat propped up on his hotel bed, the TV tuned to the sports channel and muted. "I can't put my finger on it. But there's something not quite right. The prosecution's case theory is bullshit — you don't murder your wife and burn down her studio just because you run out of money — but I can't seem to figure out what our case theory should be."

"Case theory?" Kat laughed over the phone. "You are such a fucking lawyer sometimes. How about the truth is your case theory?"

"Well, that's just it," Brunelle answered. "I don't know what the truth is. If I'm going to tell the jury Jeremy didn't do it, they're damn well gonna want to know who did. So I need to get them another suspect, but I don't have an entire police department to find one for me. This defense attorney thing kinda sucks."

Another laugh. "I don't know, David. You seem to be having a pretty good time, all things considered. Matt better watch out or he'll be trying cases against you when you get back to Seattle."

"Not likely," Brunelle replied. "Although that reminds me. I should check in with him tomorrow. Just to see how things are going.

I don't want them to forget about me."

"Mmm, don't worry, Mr. Brunelle," Kat purred. "You're pretty unforgettable."

Brunelle felt his heart quicken. "Oh. Well. Wow. Thanks. You too." Then he thought for a moment. "You home alone tonight?"

"Mm-hmm," came another low purr. "Lizzy's spending the night at a friend's. So I'm all alone and missing you. You've been gone too long."

And for the first time since he'd arrived in California, Brunelle felt homesick. Well, something-sick anyway. "You're killing me. Maybe I should fly home tonight or something."

Kat laughed. "Tonight? No, don't hurry. By the time you got here, I will have taken matters into my own hands anyway."

Brunelle groaned. "You're coming back again soon, right?"

"Yeah. Two weeks. If it's bad now, think how bad it'll be in thirteen days."

Brunelle didn't want to think about that.

"But," Kat said, "think how great it'll be on day number fourteen."

Now that was something Brunelle was glad to think about. He smiled and enjoyed his racing heart. "I miss you."

"I miss you too," Kat replied. Then, "It's getting late. I should go. And you should get some rest. I can tell you've got big plans for tomorrow."

Brunelle shrugged. "I have plans, but I'm not sure how big they are."

"What are your plans, Mr. Brunelle? I want to know what you're doing while I'm carving into a day's worth of dead bodies."

Brunelle laughed despite the darkness of the comment. Or maybe because of it. Being a homicide prosecutor could screw with your head. It was nice to have someone even more screwed.

"I have a phone call to make," he answered. "And then some

people to visit."

  "Sounds mysterious," Kat said. "Think of me."

  "I will," Brunelle answered. And he definitely wasn't lying.

CHAPTER 11

"Matt Duncan." Brunelle's boss answered the phone with his usual amicability. It reminded Brunelle to be grateful he had a boss he could also call a friend.

"Hey, Matt. It's Dave. Just checking in."

Brunelle was still in his hotel room. He'd slept through the hotel's breakfast. He was usually an early riser—or at least didn't usually sleep too late—but he'd had trouble getting to sleep after hearing that purr in Kat's voice. To make up for the late start, he began his day with the one thing he could do while he was still in his t-shirt and boxers.

"Well, that's nice of you," Duncan replied. "But no need. Everything's under control."

Brunelle was glad to hear that. Mostly. It would have been okay to be missed a little bit too. "Oh yeah? Well. That's good. How's Yamata holding up?"

"Great," Duncan enthused. "Fantastic. What was that word you used to describe her?"

Brunelle winced. "Exquisite," he nearly groaned.

"Yeah," Duncan agreed. "Exquisite. She's really taken the bull by the horns. She worked up every case, even got a few things done that you hadn't quite gotten to yet."

Brunelle felt stung. And a little embarrassed. "Hadn't gotten to yet? Like what?"

"Oh, nothing major, Dave. Don't worry. Just little things. Like one case needed a witness list filed. Stuff like that, you know?"

He did know. But he didn't like people correcting his work. She was supposed to be baby-sitting them, not taking them over. "Which case?"

"I'm not sure," Duncan replied. "She said it was coming up for trial next month, but subpoenas hadn't gone out yet, so I gave the okay to do up the witness list."

"McAllister," Brunelle guessed the defendant's name. He knew which case was coming up for trial next month. He also knew why he hadn't done subpoenas yet.

"Yeah, I think that was it," Duncan confirmed. "The McAllister case."

"Well, see, that one's going to settle," Brunelle felt compelled to explain. "His lawyer accepted the Murder Two offer. We just haven't set the plea date yet."

"Oh, okay," Duncan answered. "Well, Yamata didn't seem to know that. Maybe McAllister changed his mind. Anyway, she felt there was a need to send out a witness list and subpoenas, so I okayed it."

Brunelle surrendered a begrudging nod, a gesture entirely worthless over the telephone.

"But, yes, anyway," Duncan filled up the ensuing silence, "she's doing a bang up job. I may even let her keep a case or two when you get back."

Brunelle was too stunned to protest immediately. *Take my cases?*

Duncan took advantage of his hesitation by turning the conversation. "You are coming back, right? You haven't fallen in love with the dark side or anything, have you?"

Brunelle laughed. "Oh, no. No chance of that. Your friend Dombrowski made sure of that."

"Uh-oh," Duncan replied. "For the record, he wasn't really a friend. More like an acquaintance. What's wrong with him?"

"He's just a true believer is all," Brunelle replied. "He told me every prosecutor in San Francisco is dirty."

"Just San Francisco?" Duncan laughed.

"Well, I'm pretty sure he thinks you and I are dirty too, but he was polite enough not to say anything."

"I bet they knew you were a prosecutor the moment you stepped in their office," Duncan said.

Or a sex offender. "I bet you're right." Then, to steer away from that particular embarrassing memory, Brunelle said, "You know what really sucks about being a defense attorney?"

"Defending guilty people?" Duncan ventured.

"Well, I'm telling myself that I don't have that particular problem," Brunelle replied. "No, what really sucks is not having the entire police department to do whatever follow up investigation I want done."

"So do it yourself," Duncan answered. "You know how the game works. Besides, you're still really a prosecutor. Turn on that good guy charm and they'll be helping you anyway. Especially if your guy really is innocent."

There was silence for a few seconds as Brunelle considered the advice. But Duncan followed up with the other part of his statement.

"Is he really innocent, Dave?"

That mattered. It mattered to Duncan. He was a prosecutor. And it mattered to Brunelle. Present circumstances notwithstanding, he was a prosecutor too.

Brunelle shrugged. "I hope so, Matt. I hope so."

CHAPTER 12

The office of Overstreet and Stephenson, Cosmetic Surgeons, was tucked between the picturesque Pacific Heights neighborhood and downtown San Francisco. And of course, it wasn't called Overstreet and Stephenson, or even Stephenson and Overstreet. It was 'Adonis Image Studios.'

Brunelle stepped off the elevator onto the seventh floor of the modern office building and had no trouble spying the enormous sign for Adonis Image Studios that practically mugged anyone daring to get off the elevator on that floor. There was also a small sign suggesting an orthodontist at the other end of the hallway, but clearly Adonis took up most of the floor. It looked like they were doing well. But then, as any cosmetic surgeon knew, looks can be deceiving.

Brunelle opened the office door and stepped into a palatial waiting room, complete with a black marble floors, recessed mood lighting, and a half dozen aquariums filled with tropical salt-water fish. There were three men seated together near the receptionist. They looked up as Brunelle's heels clicked against the floor on his way to the absolutely stunning receptionist. Blond hair, blue eyes, pouty lips, large chest. She was like a billboard for the business. Or a sample catalog.

"Hello," she greeted him. Her teeth were bright white and perfectly straight. Brunelle wondered whether Adonis had a kick-back arrangement with the orthodontist down the hall. "How can I help you today, sir?"

Brunelle liked that question. Very effusive. It matched her appearance. He wondered if she didn't perhaps absolutely despise her job. That would be ironic. "Hi. I was wondering if Dr. Overstreet might be available?"

The smile didn't budge. "Do you have an appointment?"

Brunelle smiled too. He enjoyed a battle. Even when he knew he was going to lose. "No, but I think he'll want to talk to me."

She blinked once, her smile unwavering. "Is this for a consultation?"

Brunelle was a bit taken aback. He didn't need any work done. He didn't think he did anyway. "No, no. I represent his partner, Jeremy Stephenson. I need to talk to him about some of the business aspects of their practice."

That did it. The smile shattered and her pretty blue eyes darted to the men sitting within earshot. "Uh, Dr. Overstreet isn't in right now." She glanced over at her computer monitor and made a few clicks. "Can you come back at five?" she asked in a lowered voice. "His last appointment is at four forty-five."

Brunelle's smile returned. He thought he might just have won the battle. "Absolutely. Thank you. I'll see you at five."

He turned to leave, a bounce in his step from his apparent victory, and nodded to the stocky men in dark suits whose upturned and unpleasant faces obviously would benefit from the services provided by Dr. Overstreet.

* * *

The rest of Brunelle's day was less successful than even that small victory.

He went next to the medical examiner's office. It was in the

Hall of Justice, just like the police department, but it was closer to the door. And he was really missing Kat after staring at a Barbie doll receptionist. Somehow, he thought the sight of dissected cadavers might ease his ache.

It didn't.

Actually, he didn't get to find out. He never made it out of the lobby. Brunelle asked the receptionist to speak with the doctor who'd conducted the Vanessa Stephenson autopsy. He didn't really expect it to work, so he wasn't surprised when, really, it didn't.

"Mr. Brunelle," came the icy greeting of the assistant medical examiner who emerged to greet him. She was short, wiry, and plain, with a sharp nose and beady eyes. Brunelle immediately didn't like her. The feeling was obviously mutual. "I'm Dr. Sylvia Tuttle. What do you want?"

"Nice to meet you," Brunelle lied. "I was wondering if you had time to discuss the Vanessa Stephenson autopsy."

Dr. Tuttle shook her head sharply, sending her straight brown hair swinging. "I don't talk to defense attorneys. You have my autopsy report. If you need anything more, contact the prosecutor's office."

"I'm not going to try to trick you or anything," Brunelle insisted. "I just had a few questions to make sure I understood your findings properly."

"I'm sure you understood them," Dr. Tuttle replied. "Or maybe you didn't. I don't know. That's your problem. But I don't need to speak with you and I'm not going to. I only came out to tell you that personally so you would believe it and not badger my receptionist."

"I wouldn't badger her," Brunelle defended. "I'm actually a prosecutor—"

"I know," the medical examiner interrupted. "Jim called me. But you're not a prosecutor on this case. You're the defense attorney and I don't talk to defense attorneys."

Brunelle stood mute for a moment, unsure what to say. It didn't matter; Dr. Tuttle was done. "Goodbye, Mr. Brunelle," she announced and then turned on her heel and disappeared back into the bowels of the medical examiner's office.

Brunelle looked at the receptionist he never would have badgered. She just smiled and shrugged. Brunelle smiled back and shrugged himself.

Maybe the detective would be more helpful.

* * *

Or maybe not.

Detective Frank Ayala was the lead detective on the Stephenson case. He was tall and barrel-chested, with tanned skin, a full black moustache, and a clean-shaven head. He seemed like a nice enough guy, and Brunelle could easily imagine working with him on a case. But not this case. Westerly had called him too.

"I'm sorry. Mr. Brunelle. If you want to interview me, you'll have to arrange it through the prosecutor."

"I don't want to interview you," Brunelle said as amicably as he could. "I just want to talk to you. I have a couple questions about the investigation."

"Sorry, sir," Ayala said, and he did seem sorry. "If you want to talk with me, I want the prosecutor present. You'll need to work through him."

Brunelle ran a hand over his gray-flecked head. "Really, it's just a couple friendly questions. I'm not trying to trick you. I'm not going to criticize your investigation. I just need to get a couple things clear in my head."

Ayala crossed his thick arms. Obviously, there was a limit to his patience. "I said I can't talk to you, Mr. Brunelle. Contact the prosecutor. Schedule something. Get me at a conference table with the prosecutor sitting there, and I'll answer any question you ask. But not here and not now."

Brunelle considered arguing some more, but realized it would be both unproductive and unprofessional. And just kind of jerky. "Okay," he capitulated. "Thanks, detective. I appreciate your time."

Ayala nodded. "Good luck, Mr. Brunelle." Then he grinned. "But not too much. I still want you to lose."

Brunelle grinned back. "Well, maybe you won't after we finally talk."

* * *

Brunelle decided to make his next effort more comfortable, at least for him. And more opaque. Westerly had warned the M.E. and the detective. Brunelle hoped he hadn't thought to call the insurance agent.

So he indulged in a tall mocha and a table at the back, then took out his phone and dialed National Fidelity Insurance and Casualty of St. Louis, Missouri.

It took a few transfers and vague assertions about being the lawyer 'assigned' to the arson claim, but eventually Brunelle found himself talking to Mike Wolfram, Senior Claims Adjuster.

"Okay, okay, okay," Wolfram said, apparently looking through an actual paper file. "Let me see, let me see. Okay, yes. I have it here. Right in front of me. Yes. Yes, we paid that claim, but only in part. The other part is still pending."

That was interesting. "Of course," Brunelle replied vaguely. "I was wondering if you could tell me why."

Brunelle could hear pages being turned.

"Let's see, let's see, let's see. Okay, yes, here we go. We pended it because of intervening criminal action."

"Intervening criminal action?"

"Correct," Wolfram said. "That means somebody committed a crime so we don't have to pay. Or least we might not have to, depending on the outcome of the case."

"Ah, okay," Brunelle said. "That makes sense. And what crime exactly?"

Brunelle knew of course, but his goal was to see what info the insurance company had. He'd learned along the way that sometimes people said things to the insurance company to get their money that they declined to tell law enforcement. Money talks. And it makes people talk too.

"Um, um, um," Wolfram muttered. More pages turning. "Looks like arson. We see that a lot." Then he kept reading. "Oh! Oh, and murder. Oh my, murder. Yes, we definitely decline claims when there's been a murder. We don't insure against murder. No one insures against murder."

"Of course not," Brunelle replied. Seemed like a sound business policy. "So you've placed part of the claim on hold. Could you tell me who the beneficiaries were?"

Even if he couldn't get all the details, just the identity of the beneficiaries could be helpful. And if it wasn't, well, then, he could do what defense attorneys always did with unhelpful information. Bury it.

"Excuse me?" Wolfram said. "What did you just ask?"

Brunelle sipped from his mocha. "I asked if you could tell me who made the claim."

"I, I thought that's who you represented," Wolfram said. "I thought you were the lawyer for the beneficiary whose claim we pended."

Brunelle set his drink down. He knew the call was about to end. "Uh, no," he admitted. It was one thing to be vague. But he wasn't going to lie. Not only was it unethical, it was unprofessional. The Bar looked down on lawyers committing fraud. Again, Jeremy Stephenson wasn't worth his bar card. "I represent Jeremy Stephenson, the man accused of murdering his wife and burning down the building." Then to make sure it was perfectly clear. "I'm his criminal defense attorney."

"Oh! Oh! No, I'm sorry. I didn't understand." The papers were loudly being stuffed back into whatever files Wolfram had pulled them from. "I can't talk to you. I shouldn't be talking to you. I shouldn't have said anything at all. I didn't understand."

Brunelle actually felt bad for his deception. "Don't worry, Mr. Wolfram. You didn't tell me anything I couldn't already have guessed. But can I ask one more question?"

Wolfram hesitated. "Well, I don't know. I mean, no, I don't think so, but maybe. It depends on the question."

Brunelle nodded. That made sense. He didn't really need the answer, but he was curious. "Would you talk to me if I were the prosecutor?"

Wolfram paused again. "Well, um, no, actually. We'll talk to the lawyer for the insured. But no, we wouldn't talk to you and we wouldn't talk to the prosecutor either."

Well, that was something. "Thank you, Mr. Wolfram. Have a nice day."

"Um, oh, uh, well, you too, I guess."

'I guess.' Brunelle had to chuckle. Then he took a long drink of his coffee and realized he was pretty well fucked.

* * *

But it was about to go from unsatisfying to worse.

Brunelle had to admit he didn't know how to investigate as a defense attorney. He was willing to do it himself—he had enough time with only one case and a girlfriend a thousand miles away—but clearly he didn't know what he was doing. Still, he knew enough to know that when he didn't know something he should ask someone who did. And he thought he probably had time to visit his expert on being a defense attorney before getting back to Adonis & Overstreet, Inc., by five.

Dombrowski's office was in Haight-Ashbury. Trendy and

eclectic, but safe, mostly. But getting there took Brunelle through some less savory neighborhoods, which at first made him think the thugs who stopped him in the street a few blocks from Dombrowski's office were just run-of-the-mill muggers. Until he recognized them from the Adonis waiting room.

Once he was sufficiently surrounded and had stopped walking, one of the men stepped forward. "You represent Jeremy Stephenson, yes?"

He had an accent. Russian, maybe? Brunelle wasn't sure. Something Eastern European, he thought.

"Uh, yes." Brunelle didn't see any point in lying. He didn't understand what was going on, so he couldn't guess what answers were best to give. He might as well go with the truth.

The man—an especially ugly man, with a pug nose, pock-marked cheeks, and a gold tooth—stepped forward and punched Brunelle right in the gut.

Brunelle wasn't ready for it. He probably should have been, but he wasn't. He dropped to his knees and grabbed his stomach. The man followed up with a blow to his face. It actually hurt less than the gut punch, the fist glancing off his left cheek bone,

"Remind Mr. Stephenson he still owes his debt," the man warned Brunelle. "And he is no safer inside than you are out on the street."

Brunelle raised a hand to his swelling cheek and looked up at the ugly man and his two burly back-ups. "Don't worry. I'll definitely tell him."

CHAPTER 13

Kylie pressed a cold washcloth against the bruise swelling on Brunelle's cheek. There was a small cut too, so it stung. He clenched his jaw against the pain. He wasn't going to let Kylie see him wince.

"You seem okay," she said. "You into this stuff or something?"

Brunelle cocked looked askance at her. "Into getting hit?"

"Mm-hmm," she confirmed with a slight nod and an inviting eyebrow.

Before he thought, he said, "No." Her disappointed expression made him regret his quick response. She took his hand and raised it to the washcloth so he could hold it there himself. She stood up and returned to her work station.

Dombrowski stepped over to distract Brunelle from his unexpected and confused disappointment. "What happened?"

Dombrowski's question succeeded in drawing his attention away from Kylie. "Uh, I'm not sure. I guess I need to ask my client a few more questions."

"You know he's going to lie to you, right?"

Brunelle nodded. "Yeah, I've got that part down. Thanks. I'm hoping visible injuries will help motivate some honesty."

Dombrowski frowned. "I wouldn't expect it. So what the hell were you doing today?"

Brunelle shrugged. "Investigation. I started at my guy's office, then tried the M.E. and the detective, but that didn't go very well. I was walking here to ask your advice when these guys just showed up out of nowhere."

Dombrowski stared at him for several moments. "You really have no idea what you're doing, do you?"

Brunelle felt an urge to argue the point. But it passed. "No. I have no fucking idea what I'm doing."

Kylie laughed. He looked at her and the disappointment he'd seen earlier had been replaced with some admiration for his honesty. Brunelle looked back up to Dombrowski. He stepped over to his desk and returned with a business card. "You need an investigator to do this for you. Sophia is the best."

Brunelle took the card. *Sophia Farinelli, Private Investigator.*

"The best, huh?" he questioned.

Dombrowski shrugged. "Well, better than you anyway."

Kylie laughed again. Brunelle did too.

* * *

Brunelle didn't know if Sophia Farinelli was the best private investigator in San Francisco, but she had to be the hottest. Her office was just a few blocks from Dombrowski's. She'd taken Dombrowski's call—because he sent her a lot of business—and had agreed to meet with Brunelle that afternoon. So an hour later, his cheek only a little bit numb, he walked into Sophia's office and tried to remember why he'd come over in the first place.

It wasn't her long brown hair. It wasn't her tight, curvy body. It wasn't the expensive, edgy clothing she wore, or the scent of her perfume—at once fresh and dangerous. It was her face. She had an absolutely perfect face. She could have been a model. Hell, she probably had been. It was like looking at an artist's rendition of perfection in the female face.

He was mesmerized. She was amused.

"Andy says you're really a prosecutor," she started after the introductions. Her office was decorated in a way that somehow not only matched but accentuated her vaguely exotic beauty.

"Uh-huh," he replied, trying—but failing—not to stare at her face, tracing every contour with his eyes.

"What brings you here to play defense attorney?"

"Hm? Oh, um. I'm defending someone."

"Who?"

"Jeremy Stephenson," he answered, totally without really answering. Her cheeks looked like they'd been carved from the finest marble.

"And who is he to you?"

That succeeded in breaking the trance. "Oh. Right. Um, he's the ex-husband of," he hesitated—his natural tendency in the presence of an attractive woman, but one he actually managed to overcome, "my girlfriend. He's my girlfriend's ex-husband."

Brunelle realized there was no way in hell Dombrowski hadn't told her that.

"She's a very lucky woman," Sophia said, a smile showing she'd seen the trance break. She was likely used to men losing their faculties around her. She'd quickly managed to bring him back to reality. Maybe she really was the best.

"So what are we doing first?" she asked.

And Brunelle, to his credit, didn't even think of an inappropriately sexual response. "Gary Overstreet," he answered. "My client's business partner."

Then he rose a delicate finger to his cheek. "But first, I need to talk to my client."

CHAPTER 14

Brunelle sat in the cramped jail meeting room, staring at the empty glass in front of him, barely able to see his reflection, and hoping the bruise on his cheek was more visible than it seemed in the glass. He wanted Jeremy to feel bad, and for more than one reason.

The jailer opened the door at the other end of the room and in walked Jeremy Stephenson. He looked a bit confused and sat down opposite Brunelle uneasily. "Hey, Dave," he started. "This is a nice surprise. Did we have a meeting scheduled? I think I might be starting to lose track of things."

Brunelle shook his head. He didn't return Jeremy's nervous smile. "No, nothing scheduled. I need to talk to you. Something came up yesterday."

Jeremy raised an encouraging eyebrow. "Oh yeah? What's that?"

Brunelle pointed to his cheek.

Jeremy leaned forward and squinted through the glass. "Ouch. That might leave a scar."

Always the plastic surgeon, Brunelle thought.

"What happened?" Jeremy asked.

"I got punched," Brunelle explained, "by a Russian guy. Three of them actually."

What color Jeremy had left after several weeks without sunshine drained from his face.

"We need to talk," Brunelle said.

Jeremy nodded, but looked down.

"What's going on, Jeremy?"

When Jeremy just kept looking at the jail floor, Brunelle pressed him. "I need to know. I don't mind getting punched every now and then. Hell, I even had someone suggest I look into it more. But I can't defend you if I don't know what's going on. *Everything* that's going on."

Jeremy nodded again and took a deep sigh. He looked up at Brunelle, but hesitated again.

Brunelle knew from his work that, despite the best efforts of church and state over the centuries, the most powerful human motivator was still self-interest. "There might be a defense in there, Jeremy. Something I can use. It might not seem like it to you, but you're not a lawyer. And if it comes out in the middle of trial, the prosecutor may be able to twist it before I have a chance to react. He's a lawyer too. And he wants to put you in prison for the rest of your life."

An expression of near-conviction flashed over Jeremy's features.

Brunelle leaned forward. "Help me help you."

Jeremy sighed again. He nodded a few more times. "Okay," he finally said. "It's kind of hard to admit."

"Jeremy," Brunelle modulated his voice from lawyer to friend, "you're in jail facing murder charges. It doesn't get harder than that."

A small smile crept into the corner of Jeremy's mouth. "Yeah, I guess you're right. Still…"

Brunelle decided he'd pushed enough. Jeremy was about to tell him. The best thing was to stay quiet and let Jeremy fill the silence.

"Vanessa was really excited about her studio," Jeremy started. It didn't seem really on point, but Brunelle knew people often took the long way around when telling a story. He settled in. "It wasn't just a dance studio either. They were teaching aerobics, Zumba, you name it. She was making all these contacts with different art groups in town. She wanted to bring in some African drumming and Brazilian capoeira and Chinese tai chi. She really had big plans."

Jeremy dropped his gaze for a moment. The excitement he'd briefly shown when talking about his late wife's dreams faded when he turned to the realities of the situation.

"But it takes a while to get something like that off the ground. Gary and I didn't start with a professionally decorated office near downtown. We built our practices over years, separately, only becoming partners a few years ago, after we'd established our reputations and our client bases. Vanessa didn't want to wait that long. I didn't want her to have to wait that long. I don't even know if she could have. One face-lift will pay the rent for six months. Throw in a tummy-tuck or some liposuction and we can pay the receptionist for three months. It adds up quick.

"But dance classes? Drums and tai chi? There's no money in that. Not in this town. Do you have any idea how expensive rent is? And a studio requires a lot of square feet. It's not a hot dog stand or even a jewelry store. It's big. And the people who want to do that stuff, they're the artsy types, you know? Not the bankers and doctors. It's the starving artists and their urchin kids. Do you know how many families promised to pay next week, or next month? You can't do that with the landlord, though. Or the power company. Or the city tax department."

He paused and shoved a hand into his hair. "It just wasn't working."

"So you borrowed some money from a loan shark to keep it

afloat?" Brunelle guessed.

But Jeremy shook his head. "No. I borrowed money from a loan shark to replace the money I'd taken out of Adonis. I drained those accounts. I can do that. I'm an equal partner. Me and Gary, we both own one hundred percent of the assets. But that doesn't mean Gary would have gone along with that. When we merged, I took care of the books, at least the day-to-day. We have an accounting firm too. They do quarterly audits. I knew they would find the hole I'd dug, so I borrowed some cash to fill the hole until the audit was over. I figured I could pay it back after the audit, out of our accounts again. By then, maybe, Vanessa's studio would be on its feet a bit. I don't know."

He shrugged. "I guess I knew it wouldn't work, but she was so excited about that studio. It made her so happy. I wanted her to be happy. She was at that studio all of the time, just working so hard and trying to make it a success. I hadn't seen her that happy, that passionate in so long. Almost since we met. It was nice. I wanted to support that."

"So why didn't you pay the money back?"

Jeremy looked up, surprised by the question. "I got arrested. Vanessa was murdered and the studio was burned to the ground. I never got the chance."

Brunelle thought through what he'd just been told. "So, the Adonis accounts are in order? No money is missing?"

Jeremy nodded. "Right. If you look closely, there are a series of withdrawals as I tried to prop up her studio, then a large deposit just before the quarterly audit. But the bottom line is what it's supposed to be."

"So unless the accountant alerted your partner to the irregularities," Brunelle surmised, "he probably doesn't know about this."

"Gary's a nice guy," Jeremy said, "and a hell of a surgeon. But he doesn't like to be bothered with the money stuff. He's very successful. He's always had enough money, so he doesn't worry too much about it as long as his kids' private school tuition is paid."

Brunelle rubbed his chin.

"You know this is just more motive to kill her and burn the place down for the insurance money?"

Jeremy sighed and nodded. "That's why I didn't tell you."

Brunelle nodded too. "I'm probably going to have to tell your partner."

Jeremy cast his eyes down and dropped his shoulders. "I know."

"But not yet," Brunelle said.

Jeremy looked up, askance.

"I bet he knows more than you think," Brunelle explained. "Let's see what he lets slip. And what he tries to cover up."

CHAPTER 15

The talk with Jeremy had taken long enough that Brunelle had to call and reschedule his meeting with Gary Overstreet. It was just as well though, because it gave Sophia time to check her calendar and schedule a time that worked for all three of them. Brunelle definitely wanted Sophia there for this interview and not just because he wanted to see how a plastic surgeon would react to someone who was naturally more beautiful than anything he could do with a scalpel.

They met at the Adonis office. He almost didn't recognize her when she walked in. The long brown hair had transformed to a platinum up-do. The clothing style was totally different. Rather than sultry gypsy, it was smoldering librarian. But it was the same face beneath the expertly applied make-up.

"Hey, Dave," she said casually as she joined him in the waiting room. "This should be interesting. Let me do the talking."

Brunelle was a bit surprised. They had discussed the situation over the phone. Sophia was pretty well briefed on the areas Brunelle wanted to explore, but somehow he'd imagined himself asking the questions and Sophia taking notes.

"Why?" he asked.

She just smiled, those perfect lips parting to reveal her perfect teeth. "Really?"

Brunelle thought for a moment, then relented. "Never mind. I'll just sit back and enjoy the show."

Sophia winked. "Me too."

* * *

Overstreet was staring at Sophia the entire time she unpacked her laptop and supplies in the Adonis consultation room, examining her features while his own betrayed admiration, curiosity, and professional jealousy. Brunelle was already enjoying the show. He unpacked his legal pad and leaned back in his chair.

"Thank you for agreeing to meet with us, Dr. Overstreet," Sophia began. "This shouldn't take too long. We just have a few specific areas to cover."

"Of course, Ms. Farinelli," Overstreet replied, still staring at her impeccable cheek bones. For his part, he was a good looking man. He was tan, with muscles under his shirt and a whitened smile. Interestingly, he was completely bald on top, leaving a close cropped ring of black hair over his ears and around the back of his head. Brunelle would have expected hair-plugs from someone who made a living off of other people's vanity. He appreciated the irony.

"I'll do whatever I can," Overstreet said, "to help Jeremy."

"That's good to hear," Sophia replied, her eyes cast down at her keyboard, showing off the sparkling gold eye shadow. "He could use your help."

Overstreet finally tore his eyes from Sophia to glance over at Brunelle. Brunelle nodded to confirm Sophia's assertion, but elected not to ruin the effect by actually speaking.

"Could you please start," Sophia asked, still without looking up, "with the nature of your business relationship with Jeremy? Is it a partnership, an L.L.C., or some other arrangement? And how long have you been partners?"

Overstreet nodded. It was an easy question. Factual. Perfect for getting him to start talking.

"It's a professional services corporation. It functions like a partnership, but given the nature of our services, we were required to form the P.S.C. Jeremy and I are the only owners. All income goes to the corporation, then passes directly to us without tax liability for the business. It's kind of half way between a true corporation and a true partnership."

Sophia nodded. Her downcast eyes made her seem coquettish. Certainly approachable. Even more attractive. Brunelle knew Overstreet was eating it up. He'd tell her anything she asked. No wonder Dombrowski said she was the best.

"Do you split the profits fifty-fifty then?"

Overstreet shook his head. "No, that wouldn't really be fair, if one of us was bringing in more clients or doing more expensive procedures. No, we have an accounting firm that keeps track of that for us and we each draw our share quarterly. In the meantime, we also have a slush fund for unexpected expenses that might come up. We pay that back when the quarterly draw hits. I've done that once when my car died and I needed a down payment on a new one. I don't think Jeremy's ever done anything like that."

Think again, Brunelle grinned to himself.

"Do you check the books or let the accountants do that?"

"The accountants," Overstreet was quick to dismiss the question. "That's why we hired them."

"So if there were any irregularities in the accounts, you wouldn't know about them unless the accountants told you?"

Overstreet leaned forward, his expression finally shifting from the bliss of being the presence of an attractive woman. "Is there a problem with the accounts?"

Sophia finally looked up. Slowly. With a big blink of her long, mascaraed eyelashes. "Don't worry, Mr. Overstreet. I'm just asking standard questions."

Brunelle noticed she didn't say, 'No.'

"What was your relationship," Sophia lowered her eyes and pressed on, "with Jeremy's wife Vanessa?"

That question also impacted Overstreet's features. And made him forget all about the irregularities in the accounts.

"What do you mean exactly?" he stammered.

Brunelle supposed Sophia hadn't really meant anything by it. It was his response that held meaning.

"Did you ever meet her?" Sophia asked. "Did you hang out with her socially? Or was she just your partner's wife?"

"Oh." Overstreet relaxed a bit. "I see what you mean. I met her of course. We did things socially. Barbeques or whatever. I'm married too. Two young kids. So our wives knew each other. She and Jeremy didn't have any kids, so we didn't do those things families with kids do. Swimming lessons and stuff. But yes, we spent time together."

"Was she faithful to him?"

Now that was a bit blunt, Brunelle thought. Unexpected too. Which was probably good. Overstreet didn't expect it either.

"Of course," he said rather too quickly. Then, he caught himself. "I mean, as far as I know. I guess I don't really know. I think so. She never gave me any reason to think otherwise."

"Were you looking to think otherwise?" Sophia asked, lowering her voice one half notch. A bit of the sultry gypsy after all.

Overstreet sat up straight in his chair and cast a narrowed glance between Brunelle and Sophia. "Now, look here. If you're suggesting that I was having an affair with Vanessa, you are sadly mistaken. I would never—"

Brunelle put his hand up. "We're not suggesting anything, Dr. Overstreet. We're asking. Someone killed Vanessa and Jeremy's life is hanging in the balance. We can't avoid asking hard questions just because it might be socially awkward. If the answer is no, then just say, 'No.'"

Overstreet crossed his arms and nodded begrudgingly. "No."

"Good," Brunelle said. "Glad that's cleared up."

He looked back to Sophia and nodded. She smiled at him then turned back to Overstreet. "Dr. Stephenson took nearly fifty thousand dollars out of your corporate account to pay for Vanessa's failing business venture. He replaced the money with a loan from some loan sharks and intended on repaying them by taking money out again after the quarterly audit."

Overstreet's jaw practically hit the floor. But he believed her. "Is that why he killed her?"

Again, it wasn't Sophia's question that held meaning, it was Overstreet's response.

"So you do think he murdered his wife?" Sophia asked.

Overstreet hesitated. "Uh, well, no. I mean, that's not what I meant. I mean, I don't know."

Brunelle frowned, but nodded. That was probably the fairest answer.

"But I don't understand," Overstreet went on. "Why would he need to take money out of Adonis? Vanessa had her own partner, Laura Mayer. And she's loaded."

Brunelle looked at Sophia, his surprise offset by her apparent lack of it.

"He didn't mention that," Brunelle said.

"Of course not," Sophia answered.

She turned back to Overstreet. "Thank you, doctor. I think we're done for now." Then she looked again to Brunelle and smiled that perfectly formed, lipstick-stained smile. "I believe we have someone else we need to go see."

CHAPTER 16

Laura Mayer lived in a downtown condo with a view of San Francisco Bay and the Golden Gate Bridge. She was likely in her mid-fifties, but it was hard to tell because she clearly took care of herself. She had that runner's physique and a healthy, sun-kissed complexion. Her home reflected her sensibilities, decorated with a mix of original art and nature objects. Most of the art was of women—strong independent women, or women supporting each other. Like she'd done for Vanessa, Brunelle thought.

Her straight blonde-gray hair was cut at jaw-length and she was wearing a casual, but classy shorts and tank-top combo. If she was troubled by the appearance of an attorney and a private investigator at her door, she didn't show it. Instead, she threw her door wide and invited them in.

"Thank you for taking the time to meet with us today," Brunelle started as they walked into the sitting area. "As I mentioned on the phone, we represent Jeremy Stephenson in the alleged murder of his wife."

"Vanessa," Laura said as they sat down and she began pouring them tea from the tea pot she'd filled while they drove over. "She had a name. Let's use it."

"Of course," Brunelle replied. He felt an urge to apologize and explain that he really was a prosecutor, but that would have led to an explanation about how not only was he representing Vanessa's alleged murderer, but he was dating the ex-wife of that murderer. Something in Laura Mayer's demeanor suggested that information wouldn't prove helpful to his cause. "You knew Vanessa?"

Laura handed out the tea to her guests. She had very nice china. "Yes. We were friends and business partners."

"The dance studio?" Brunelle confirmed. This time, Sophia would be taking the back seat. They didn't suppose she would have the same disorienting effect on Laura as she'd had on Overstreet.

"Oh, Mr. Brunelle," Laura said as she scooted back in her seat and raised her teacup to her lips. "It was much more than a dance studio."

"Is that right?" Brunelle replied. He was more than happy to let her talk about it. It was how she was connected to the case. If he could get her talking, she'd likely offer information he wouldn't even know to ask for.

"Oh yes," Laura replied. "It was the culmination of a dream."

Brunelle glanced around the condo. It looked like she'd culminated just fine without a bankrupt dance studio. Laura noticed his perusal of her home.

"Not my dream, Mr. Brunelle," she explained. "Vanessa's."

Brunelle took a moment to think. Sophia stepped into the breach. "What was Vanessa's dream, Laura?"

Laura took another sip of her tea and set down the cup and saucer. "Vanessa was a beautiful soul. She was an artist and a dreamer. She saw beauty where others saw none, or rather, where others didn't even know to be looking. She was selfless and caring. She found joy in the simplest things, and she wanted to share that joy with others. Have you ever seen a person truly dance? Not repeat the steps of a waltz to music played by musicians playing the notes written by yet someone else. No, I mean a person dancing to the music inside her own soul. Vanessa danced like that. And her dream was to share that joy with anyone and everyone she could."

Brunelle listened and knew two things when she'd finished. She meant every word of it, and he didn't understand any of it. "So you helped her with that dream?"

She shrugged and picked her tea back up. "I invested in her and her dream. I believe it would have worked out if her husband hadn't..." But she trailed off.

"Jeremy," Brunelle felt compelled to say. "He has a name too."

Laura forced a tight smile. "Of course he does. And you're his lawyer. But Vanessa was my friend."

"And business partner?" Sophia confirmed. Brunelle appreciated the attempt to return the conversation to the facts, and to refine those facts.

"Yes," Laura replied. "But the business is finished."

Brunelle considered a provocative question like, 'Did her death relieve you of any financial burdens?' but thought better of it. Her affection for Vanessa seemed genuine. And her affluence was equally obvious. They had come to see whether there was reason to doubt Jeremy's claim that he'd had to drain the Adonis accounts to pay for Vanessa's studio. That goal had been accomplished. There was more than enough reason.

"Thank you for your time, Ms. Mayer," he said, setting down his tea and standing up. "We appreciate your candor."

Sophia stood up as well and Laura showed them out. Once they were down in the lobby, Sophia asked, "Are you going to confront Jeremy about all this?"

Brunelle shook his head. "No. I'm going to figure out what it all means. I don't need his lies to get in the way of that."

CHAPTER 17

Brunelle didn't visit Jeremy again for several days. He was still trying to figure out how to reconcile what his client had told him with what Overstreet and Laura had told him. Added to the mix was the ethical dilemma he faced, namely that his client had provided him with one hell of a motive for murder. As a prosecutor, he was used to having to hand over every bit of evidence and information to the defense. But as a defense attorney, not only was he not required to disclose adverse information, it would be unethical for him to do so. So it wasn't really an ethical dilemma. The ethics were clear—the 'professional ethics' anyway. But the morals of it left a bitter taste in his mouth.

Added to that frustration was the fact that he couldn't talk to anybody about it. Attorney-client privilege confined his circle of confidants to the defense team, which consisted of him, his lying client, and the most beautiful private investigator in the world.

So he was in a pissy mood when he called Kat the night before she was flying down again for a week-long visit.

"Hey, lover," she purred when the call connected. "Are you ready for a few days off?"

"I thought I was already on leave," he replied. He tried to

sound light-hearted, but he wasn't feeling it.

"Well, a few days off from your leave," Kat corrected. "I know you've been working hard. I'm looking forward to thanking you in person."

This was where Brunelle should have flirted back. They couldn't do anything over the phone of course. There wasn't an app for that quite yet. But again, he wasn't feeling it. He was feeling frustrated and irritable, and he couldn't even tell her why.

"That'll be nice," he managed to say.

"Nice?" Kat repeated. "Just nice?"

When Brunelle didn't reply, she followed up, "Are you okay, David?"

Brunelle frowned. She couldn't see it, but he supposed it was in his voice. "I'm fine. It's just been a long couple of days."

"Is the case not going well?" Kat's concern was understandable, but it just irritated him more. It reminded him he was defending her ex-husband, the father of her kid. Not really what he wanted to think about when she was trying to flirt.

"It's going fine," he insisted unconvincingly.

Kat was quiet for a few seconds. "You need someone to talk to. I know you can't talk to me. Can you talk to Matt's lawyer friend? Is there anyone else you can talk with?"

Brunelle's mind went immediately to Sophia Farinelli. It was pleasant, but it just made him feel guilty, and even less in the mood to talk with his girlfriend. He reminded himself that she was the most beautiful medical examiner in the world, but it was little help.

"No, not really," he answered. "I guess I just don't feel like talking at all sometimes."

"Like tonight," Kat said.

"Yeah," Brunelle admitted.

"That's okay," Kat replied, cheerful despite Brunelle's moroseness. "I like it sometimes when you're quiet. I'll see if I can't get you to make some noise tomorrow night."

Brunelle had to smile. "Thanks, Kat."

"I'm going to hang up now," she said. "You go pout and get it out of your system. You're a hell of a lawyer and you'll figure out whatever's bothering you."

The smile broadened.

"So I'm going to let this pass," Kat continued. "Because I'm a hell of a girlfriend and you're going to have it figured out before I get there. Right?"

Brunelle nodded. Yep, the most beautiful medical examiner in the world. "Right."

CHAPTER 18

The next morning, Brunelle didn't have it figured out yet. But he did have a few hours before Kat's plane came in. He'd offered to meet her at the gate, but she insisted on taking the hotel shuttle. It wasn't like he had a car, so why should he pay to go there and back when she could just pay once and meet him at his room? She was a big girl. A big, beautiful girl.

So what better way for Brunelle to get ready for her arrival than going to grill her ex-husband about all the lies he was feeding him?

He didn't beat around the bush when Jeremy sat down across from him.

"Okay, listen." Brunelle jabbed a finger at the glass. "Let's get a few things straight. First of all, I'm only doing this because Kat asked me to. I don't give a fuck any more whether you're guilty or innocent. Second, I'm your only hope of not dying in prison. Get that through your thick fucking skull. Third, stop fucking lying to me. Every time I talk to somebody about this case, I learn something new that you lied about. If that happens during the trial, you're fucked. Not me. You. You are fucked. You are going to prison. And you are going to be somebody's girlfriend. For the rest of your fucking life. So, either you stop lying to me and start telling me the truth, the whole truth, and nothing but the truth, or I stop visiting you, I stop talking to witnesses, and I just show up for the trial and see if I can think of any cross examination questions after the prosecutor puts on witness after witness to show how fucking guilty you are of murdering your fucking wife." Brunelle could feel his heart racing and fists clenching. It had been a long time since he'd let himself get that angry. It kind of felt good. He pointed again at Jeremy. "Understood?"

Jeremy just stared at him for several long seconds. Then he crossed his arms and leaned back. "Understood."

Brunelle exhaled and lowered his accusatory finger. He leaned back in his chair too. "Good."

"What do you want to know?" Jeremy asked.

Brunelle wasn't sure. He hadn't made a list. He decided to work backwards. "Who's Laura Mayer?"

Jeremy nodded. "What else do you want to know?"

"How much did you really take out of the accounts and what was it really for? Because Laura Mayer was paying for your wife's dance studio."

"What else?"

"Was Vanessa having an affair with Overstreet?"

That one at least produced a wince in the corner of Jeremy's eye. "Anything else?"

"Were *you* having an affair with anyone? Overstreet's wife? Laura Mayer? Your receptionist?"

It was Jeremy's turn to get angry. His chest was starting to heave and although his arms were still crossed, the muscles across his forearms were flexed. "Is that all?"

"It's a start," Brunelle replied.

Jeremy nodded several times, then uncrossed his arms and leaned forward in his chair. "I won't lie to you, Brunelle. But I'm not going to tell you everything either. Some things I won't dignify with a response. Others are none of your goddamned business. I'll tell you this: I didn't murder my wife. That's what you need to know. That's all you need to know. Now, go do your job and get me out of here."

Brunelle hadn't expected that response. He thought his 'girlfriend' threat would be sufficient to scare Jeremy into spilling his guts. Apparently he was made of sterner stuff. That was good, because if he kept playing games like that he was definitely going to prison. Still, he was making it impossible for Brunelle to do his job.

"Why should I," he asked, "if you won't help me?"

Jeremy smiled. "You said it yourself."

Brunelle cocked his head, not understanding.

"You're doing this because Kat asked you to," Jeremy said. "So I guess I'm not the only one who's fucked after all."

* * *

"You want to visit him?" Brunelle was stunned. Kat hadn't been at the hotel for five minutes and she wanted to go visit that jackass in jail? "Right now?"

Kat put her hands on her hips. She was wearing a beautiful gauzy skirt that hung to her ankles but also let him see her shapely legs underneath. It was accentuated by a tightly fitting linen blouse, unbuttoned one button too far to show off a beautiful gold and pearl necklace. She looked great. He'd thought it was for him. He wasn't sure any more.

"Visiting hours are today, David," she almost scolded. "We talked about this. I flew in on a Wednesday specifically so I could visit him right away and get it over with, then spend the rest of the week focusing on you, and us."

Brunelle ran a hand over his face. He did vaguely recall something about that. He recalled wanting to object to it, but being swayed by a purr about 'focusing on you, and us.'

He looked at his watch. Visiting hours were just about to start, and would stop in two hours. Maybe they could grab a romantic dinner afterwards. Where do you take a girl who's just visited her ex-husband in jail?

"Fine," he acquiesced. "Let's go. But I'm going to want a lot of focusing afterwards."

Kat laughed and grabbed his arm. "Of course. I want you to tell me everything you've learned and how you're going to win the case."

Brunelle sighed. "I'm not sure that's really focusing on me."

Kat looked up at him. "You have one case. Do you really have anything else to talk about?"

He thought for a moment, then sighed again. "I guess not. That's kind of depressing."

She leaned up on her tiptoes and kissed his cheek. "Don't worry. I promise I'll cheer you up later tonight."

And the thought of that cheered him up already.

* * *

She was in there a long time. That's what it felt like to Brunelle anyway. He knew they had a kid in common. He knew he was facing the very real possibility of going to prison for the rest of his life for a murder he maybe didn't commit. But really, he was standing right there, waiting in the jail lobby. Couldn't she cut it short a bit, just to make him feel better?

He shrugged and sat down on one of the plastic bench chairs. It wasn't about him, he knew. He just wished it didn't have to be about Jeremy either. Maybe he could get Westerly to switch sides or something.

"Naw," he mumbled aloud as he shook his head lightly. "Kat would never go for that."

"I'd never go for what?" she asked, walking over from the visitors' access door across the lobby.

"Uh, Chinese food," Brunelle pulled a response out of the air. "You know, for dinner."

Kat cocked her head at him. "I love Chinese. You know that. I've been looking forward to San Francisco Chinese food for the last month."

He stood up and clapped his hands. "All right then. It's settled. Chinese. Great. Okay. Let's go."

Kat reached out and took his hand. "You okay?"

Brunelle shrugged. "Yeah." He squeezed her hand. "This defense attorney thing is hard. No one wants to help you."

She squeezed back. "I do."

He smiled and looked into her eyes. "I know. That's the only reason I'm doing it."

She smiled back. "I know too. Thanks."

And suddenly he wasn't mad any more.

She pulled him toward the exit. "Let's grab an early dinner."

He definitely wasn't mad any more.

* * *

Dinner was a little awkward. He couldn't really talk about the case. Just procedural things. The upcoming trial date. The status conference. The pretrial on Friday and how useless it was since Jeremy wouldn't take any deals anyway. But no details. Kat wasn't part of the defense team, so he couldn't tell her about the accounts, or Overstreet, or how Vanessa danced with joy in her soles or whatever. She didn't seem to mind and they spent most of dinner talking about her work, and Lizzy's latest crush. He was in a band.

"Teenagers," Brunelle muttered, which only made them both laugh at him for sounding like such an old curmudgeon. By the time dinner was finished, he was in a better mood and was pretty much over his girlfriend delaying the best part of their reunion until after she spoke with her ex-husband, the lying murderer.

Then Kat delayed it further by insisting on a walk along the beach as the sun was setting. He really needed to get her back to his hotel room. It had been way too long. Spending weeks looking at

Kylie, Barbie, and Sophia hadn't helped any either.

So he was very pleasantly surprised when the sun set in earnest and right there, in the middle of the darkened beach, Kat twisted her fingers into his shirt and fell backward onto the sand, pulling him down on top of her. He was so focused on, first, trying to keep his balance, then second, not smashing his head onto hers, that she was able to grab his hips and position him in exactly the right place. He was rising quickly against her, and she let out a low moan as she pushed her hips up to him.

"Right here?" he said. "On the beach?"

"God yes," she panted in his ear, grabbing the lobe between her teeth.

"What about the sand?"

"I don't care about the sand, David," she growled. "It's been too long. I don't care if I get sand in every body cavity I have, as long as you're inside me too."

It had been too long. It wasn't what he'd imagined over the last few days—that had involved the hotel bed ...and the shower ...and the balcony. But he wasn't going to complain. And he wasn't going to last long either. There'd be time enough for the bed and shower and balcony later that night.

He slid Kat's gauzy skirt up over her hips and finally felt confident she'd worn it for him.

"I missed you," he whispered in her ear.

"I missed you too." She tipped her head back and arched her back. "Now shut up and fuck me."

CHAPTER 19

The next day was almost as perfect as the night before. Brunelle took a vacation from the case and he and Kat spent the day touring the city. Downtown. The Presidio. They skipped Alcatraz though.

It was back to work on Friday. There was a second pretrial conference, the last court date before the status conference scheduled a week before the trial. The good news was that there wasn't much to do at the pretrial. Pretrials were for negotiations, but Jeremy had said no deals, and Brunelle didn't expect Westerly to improve his offer anyway.

Turns out he was wrong.

"Manslaughter One and Arson One," Westerly offered right out of the box. He handed Brunelle a formal offer sheet with the details reduced to writing. "Ten years. It's a hell of a deal. Your guy is crazy if he rejects it."

My guy is an asshole if he rejects it, Brunelle thought. *He's an asshole anyway.*

The offer was good. Too good. Westerly had found a problem in his case.

Brunelle appraised the offer sheet, debating whether to call

Westerly on it. He couldn't think of a good reason not to. "This offer is too good, Jim. Why? If there's a problem with your case, you have to tell me under the discovery rules."

Brunelle wasn't entirely sure about that last part. It was generally true that prosecutors had to hand over any evidence that tended to show the defendant might be innocent, or that the prosecution's witnesses might be liars, but if it was just a general fear that some the witnesses might not show up, that probably didn't have to be disclosed. But this wasn't a gangland shooting with uncooperative witnesses, or a domestic violence case with a recanting victim. The witnesses were professionals and respectable citizens. They'd honor their subpoenas. No, Brunelle had read every page of the police reports. It was a circumstantial case, but the circumstantial evidence was pretty good. Too good to knock a Murder One down to a Manslaughter.

Westerly shook his head. "There's nothing wrong with my case, Dave. I've just been thinking about what you said at the last pretrial. Your guy is sympathetic. He has no history and isn't likely to do this again. All you need is one juror who buys his 'I don't know what happened' defense and the jury will hang. More likely, that one juror negotiates the verdict down from murder to manslaughter. So let's save some time and do that up front. I can get on to my other cases and you can get back to Seattle."

Brunelle frowned and looked down at the offer again. It was a hell of an offer. But Jeremy was a hell of an asshole.

"I'll talk to him," Brunelle said. "But just so you know, he's told me no deals, so you better send out your subpoenas."

* * *

Brunelle didn't go immediately to the jail. He stopped by the library first. Not because he needed to check anything out. He needed a printer. When he got to the jail and Jeremy was brought to the consultation rom, Brunelle was armed with what his defense attorney friends affectionately called a 'C.Y.A. letter.'

"More lectures?" Jeremy asked as he sat down across from Brunelle.

Brunelle shook his head. "Nope. Got a new offer from the prosecutor. I'm here to communicate it."

"I told you no deals," Jeremy snapped. "Don't you listen?"

"I listen fine," Brunelle replied evenly. "I also have an ethical obligation to communicate every offer to you." He slid the offer sheet through the thin slot at the bottom of the glass.

Jeremy pulled it through and barely glanced at it. "You know I'm going to reject it."

"Yeah, I know." Brunelle slid the C.Y.A. letter through the slat too. Then he took a pen from his suit coat pocket, unscrewed it, and slid just the interior ink-tube and point through the slat too. "So read and sign this letter and I'll be going."

Jeremy picked up the C.Y.A. letter and started reading. "What's this?"

"It's a letter that says you understand the prosecutor offered you ten years, you understand you're looking at life without parole, you understand that your attorney is advising you to accept the offer—and I am, by the way; you should take this deal—but understanding all that, you're rejecting the offer and proceeding to trial."

"And I'm supposed to sign this?"

"Yep."

"Why?"

"Because after you're convicted of first degree murder and sent off to prison, you're going to have a lot of time on your hands to think about how you should have taken this offer. This will protect me when you file a bar complaint saying you wish you'd taken that offer but your idiot lawyer told you to reject it because you'd win at trial."

Jeremy frowned. "But you're not saying that."

"I know," Brunelle replied. "But memories can shift when you're bored and hopeless. Besides, based on our interactions so far, I don't have a lot of faith in your honesty. Just sayin'."

Jeremy looked down at the letter then back up at Brunelle. "Whose side are you on?"

"Honestly?" Brunelle said, with a small shrug. "I'm on my own side. Remember, you're not worth my bar license. You don't have to sign it, but I'll have proof you at least looked at it and knew what you were doing."

Jeremy stared at Brunelle for a few seconds, then down at the letter for several seconds more. Finally he picked up the makeshift pen. "I'll sign it, Brunelle. But it really burns me up to do it."

Jeremy slid the signed letter and ink-tube back to Brunelle. Brunelle took them, reassembled the pen, then stood up to leave. The bad news was that he was going to have to try the case after all. The good news was that Jeremy's last comment had made Brunelle realize what was wrong with Westerly's case.

CHAPTER 20

It was time for a strategy session. In his usual job, Brunelle would have called the lead detective and another homicide prosecutor or two into his office. But he wasn't at his usual job. The lead detective and other prosecutors weren't going to help him. He had a new team—smaller, but dedicated. So by four o'clock Friday afternoon, he was in Dombrowski's office, along with Sophia the Great and Kylie the Suspicious.

Kat would meet him there at five to start their night on the town. He hoped Sophia and Kylie would be gone by then, although he knew he should give Kat more credit than that. She wouldn't be jealous. He'd just feel like she should be.

"Let's get started," Brunelle glanced at his watch. Dombrowski was looking out the window, a beer already in his hand. Sophia was typing something into her phone. Kylie was at the front desk; she wouldn't be directly involved, but Brunelle was still glad to see her. It reminded him, pleasantly somehow, of his mostly-healed facial bruise. "Thanks for letting me come over, Andy."

Dombrowski turned from the window. "Sure. I'm your local associated counsel, right? I suppose I ought to know something about the case."

Sophia didn't say anything. She just tapped her phone dark and put it her purse. She was brunette again, only jet black instead of her initial dark brown. Her ensemble was all black, mostly leather, and mildly distracting. It made Brunelle glad Det. Chen was a guy.

"What's up?" Dombrowski prompted.

"They offered him a manslaughter," Brunelle started. "Man One and Arson One. Ten years."

Dombrowski lifted his beer bottle. "Congratulations. That's a great resolution."

"It would be," Brunelle agreed, "but my guy rejected it."

Sophia raised a perfectly shaped eyebrow. Dombrowski was less subtle. "Are you fucking kidding me? What the hell is wrong with him?"

Brunelle shrugged. "He says he's innocent."

"Who gives a fuck?" Dombrowski said. "He's facing life. You got him ten years. The prisons are full of innocent people. But at least he'd get out before he dies."

Brunelle decided to ignore the jab about innocent people in prison. "Yeah, he gets that. But he's insistent. And I don't really feel like arguing with him any more."

Dombrowski took a swig of beer. "Well, you did your job. If you lose now, it's all on him. What did you do to get such a great offer?"

"That's just it." Brunelle raised his hands palm up. "Nothing. Sophia and I talked to a couple of people, but we didn't learn anything terribly helpful. Even if we had, Westerly had his offer all typed and prepared before I could say anything."

Dombrowski rocked his bottle absently. "Westerly? He's good. He's dirty, but he's good. He's not afraid of trial. He doesn't make offers just to make the case go away."

"So why did he make the offer?" Sophia finally joined the conversation.

"There's a problem with his case," Dombrowski said. "Something he doesn't want you to figure out. I told you he was dirty."

Brunelle wasn't sure it was dirty, exactly, but Westerly definitely didn't want him to figure it out. But he recalled the jury instruction the judges used to tell jurors the definition of 'reasonable doubt': a reasonable doubt can arise from the evidence, or the *lack* of evidence.

"There's no fire investigation report," Brunelle announced. "I double checked all the reports. They never did a full fire investigation."

"Why wouldn't they do a fire investigation?" Sophia asked. The very idea seemed to offend her own meticulousness.

"There was a body in the middle of the fire," Dombrowski answered for Brunelle. "The murder investigation took precedence. The cops probably sent the fire department away once the fire was out and the paramedics confirmed she was dead."

Brunelle nodded. "That's what I figured too."

"Can't they just do it now?" Sophia asked. "It hasn't been that long."

"It's been long enough," Brunelle replied. "Burned out building, open to the elements, trampled on by cops and insurance adjusters and maybe even homeless squatters. At this point, even if they did, I could keep it out."

"And it would draw your attention to their initial mistake," Dombrowski added.

"Well, just because you could keep it out," Sophia said, "doesn't mean there isn't useful information left behind."

Brunelle smiled. "I know."

That was what Brunelle had wanted to accomplish. Confirmation of his suspicion and agreement on his proposed course of action. And it was well before five. Mission accomplished.

Too bad Kat showed up early.

"Mr. Brunelle?" Kylie knocked on Dombrowski's office door. "There's a Dr. Anderson here to see you." She gave him an approving wink. "She says she's a medical examiner."

Brunelle stood up but before he could go out in the lobby, Kat walked into the office. Dombrowski set down his beer and extended a hand in greeting. "*The* Dr. Anderson?" he said. "Mr. Brunelle's girlfriend?"

Kat laughed as she shook his hand. "Actually, he's *my* boyfriend." Then she looked around and noticed the stunning perfection of Sophia Farinelli. Kat extended her hand to Sophia and introduced herself. "Kat."

"Sophia," the P.I. replied. "Dave was just briefing us on the case."

"Oh?" Kat cocked her head at her boyfriend. "That's funny," she teased. "He won't tell me anything. And I hired him."

Brunelle frowned slightly. "You didn't hire me. Well, okay, maybe you did. But you're not paying me, and Jeremy's the client. I already explained all that to you."

Kat gestured to Dombrowski and Sophia. "They aren't the client either," she pointed out.

"They're part of the defense team," Brunelle explained. "Sophia's my investigator and Andy's my local associated counsel."

Kat crossed her arms, then tapped her chin. "So you can tell everything to other members of the defense team?"

Brunelle nodded, glad she seemed to get it. "Yes. Exactly."

Kat definitely got it. Dombrowski and Sophia did too. It was Brunelle who didn't. But he was about to.

"I think we could use a little help on this one, Andy," Sophia said. "Don't you think we could use a consulting expert to review Dr. Tuttle's autopsy reports?"

Dombrowski smiled. "Oh, absolutely. But where, oh where,

could we find someone who has extensive experience as a medical examiner but isn't employed by the great State of California?"

Brunelle's jaw dropped. Kat's face lit up. She sure did seem to enjoy outsmarting him.

Sophia raised her hand. "Oh! I know." She turned to Kat. "Dr. Anderson, are you available to provide consultation on a pending murder case Mr. Brunelle is defending?"

"Why yes," Kat replied. "I believe I am. And my fee is very reasonable."

"Oh, excellent," Sophia laughed. "Welcome aboard. What's your fee?"

"Dinner for four," Kat replied. "And Mr. Brunelle is buying."

All eyes turned to Brunelle. He didn't like being outsmarted. But in truth, he was glad to have an excuse to tell Kat about the case. He didn't like keeping things from her.

"A very reasonable fee," he agreed with a smile. "Let's find someplace loud so we won't be overheard. We have a lot to tell our good doctor."

CHAPTER 21

The first order of business for the new defense team was the murder scene. Or at least, the arson scene. Well, the scene of the burned building and the dead body. Whether it was arson or not was open to question. And apparently, so was whether it was murder.

"Just because she was found dead inside the building doesn't mean she was murdered," Kat explained. "People die in fires all the time. The questions are: What mechanism caused the bodily functions to cease? And when did that happen in relation to the fire?"

So the next day Kat stayed back at the hotel to start reviewing the autopsy reports, while Brunelle and Sophia went to inspect what was left of Vanessa Stephenson's dance studio. Dombrowski wished them luck, but didn't come along. He had his own life to attend to. Words of encouragement and a beer on a Friday afternoon was about as far as he was willing to participate.

The studio was in the South of Market district—'SOMA' to the locals—near the slightly more well-known, and more dangerous, Tenderloin district. A large number of SOMA's blocks of sprawling warehouses had been transformed into start-up offices and artsy studios. One such studio was, or had been, 'Inner Beauty Dance and Dreams,' Vanessa's studio. Now it was a charred shell at the end of a block-length warehouse housing, among other things, a coffee shop, an art gallery, and a pho restaurant that was still closed due to the smoke damage from the fire next door.

The studio itself was closed up as best it could be, given the damage caused by both the fire and the firefighters. The back door was still locked. The front door was basically gone, chopped to pieces by a fireman's axe. Brunelle and Sophia ducked under the leftover crime scene tape and slipped in through the front door.

There wasn't much left. Whatever furnishing there might have been had been removed. But the walls were still there and the black scorches gave witness to the inferno that had consumed Vanessa's dreams.

"Not much left," Brunelle observed.

Sophia shrugged slightly even as she crouched down to inspect a melted electrical outlet. She was a redhead now, soft orange curls falling over a white knit top and floral skirt.

"What are you looking for?" he asked. Scene visits often reminded him he wasn't a cop; he was a lawyer. At least as a prosecutor, he was on the same team as the cops. But really, his skill wasn't finding clues, it was explaining the significance of those clues to twelve jurors.

"Signs of arson," she answered without looking back at him.

Brunelle hadn't done a lot of straight arsons. They were actually a pretty rare crime and he'd bypassed the hodgepodge trial unit that handled arson along with other hard-to-group crimes like extortion and perjury.

He squatted down next to her, uncertain what to look for, but willing to try anyway. "See anything?"

She turned and smiled at him. "You're not really an investigator, are you?"

Brunelle felt a slight blush. No reason to be embarrassed, but he was anyway. "I guess not. I think I'd need an empty gas can in the middle of the room."

Sophia laughed. It was the first time he'd heard her laugh. It wasn't a light airy giggle; it was a kind of a squeaky snort. Not perfect at all. For some reason, he was relieved.

"Well," she said, "there's nothing that obvious, but I think the arson is pretty clear. This wasn't an accidental fire."

She stood up. Brunelle followed suit. "How can you tell?"

She started to walk the wall, and pointed to some especially dark burn marks rising from the floor at uniform intervals toward the front of the studio. "An accelerant was used. I don't know if it was gasoline, but whoever started this fire wanted to make sure it really burned the place down."

"You can tell that?" Brunelle asked.

She turned and looked over her shoulder. It sent the red curls bouncing. "Are you questioning my abilities, sir?"

Brunelle kept his eyes from looking her up and down again. Barely. "No, ma'am. Just trying to learn a thing or two."

She smiled, but didn't quite laugh. He guessed she kept that laugh pretty tightly holstered. She turned back to the scorched walls. "Yes, I can tell that. Really, anyone with any experience in these cases could tell. It's beyond obvious. Whoever did it didn't make any effort to conceal it."

"Because they didn't know how?" Brunelle asked.

"Or because they didn't care. It's possible to disguise arson. Not perfectly, maybe, but at least to make it appear to be an accident. Squirting lighter fluid every three feet isn't one of them."

Brunelle thought about the cases he'd had involving burned down buildings. All of his had had a body inside, the reason the fire had started in the first place. A vain hope it would burn the body to disguise the cause of death.

"Sounds like the person wanted to conceal the murder."

Sophia put her hands on her hips and surveyed the room. "I'd have to agree. This wasn't done to collect insurance. It's too obvious."

Brunelle frowned. "So we can conclude that whoever started the fire also killed Vanessa."

"Seems likely," Sophia agreed.

"And he was an amateur."

"Yup."

Brunelle considered the middle-aged plastic surgeon with no criminal history sitting in the San Francisco County jail. "Damn."

CHAPTER 22

"The body is a crime scene, too," Kat explained. "Sometimes, you can tell as much about what happened from the body as you can from where it's found. Maybe more."

They were sitting in a small conference room inside the medical examiner's office. Kat, Brunelle, and Sophia. Sophia would be asking the questions, Brunelle would be listening to the answers, and Kat was there to call bullshit. It was the defense interview of Dr. Tuttle. Westerly had just arrived and the good doctor had dropped them off in the conference room while she fetched him from the lobby.

"But," Kat smacked Tuttle's autopsy report, "you have to actually look for evidence to see it. This is the most cursory autopsy report I've ever read. This is what you'd do if the police found a homeless man who died from exposure or an elderly person who died in a hospice. Not a body found in a fire. She found some potential bruising around the neck, called it strangulation, and barely did more than sign her name." Then she got a glint in her eye and a barely restrained smile pulled at the corner of her mouth. "I can't wait to rip her apart."

Brunelle put a hand up and shook his head. "Yes, you can. This isn't about calling her out on her mistakes. It's about locking her into them."

Sophia offered a knowing, even admiring smile but Kat's own grin disappeared completely. "What do you mean? Do you know how bad this report is? I could shred her on her initial observations alone."

Brunelle shook his head. "Not now." Then he looked at the clock and the door. He probably had just enough time. "Let me tell you a story. When I first started prosecuting felonies, I had this assault case, domestic violence. Nothing too bad, but the victim suffered a broken arm."

"That's nothing too bad?" Kat interrupted.

Brunelle shrugged. "We've both seen a lot worse."

Kat had to shrug too. She could hardly disagree.

"Anyway," Brunelle went on, "it happened one night after closing time. The couple was walking back to their car. They were drunk and yelling at each other, so of course all the neighbors started looking out their windows. At one point, he shoved her to the ground and she lands wrong and breaks her arm. My star witnesses are these college kids who were watching the whole thing through these windows in their front door."

"Sounds like a good case," Kat opined. "Causation for the injury and eye witnesses to the assault."

"Right," Brunelle agreed. "But here's the thing. The couple had already walked past the kids' house. They were at least two, maybe three houses down the sidewalk when he pushed her. And the windows in the front door—they were pretty small, and had these beveled edges that kind of interfered with seeing clearly. Plus it was two in the morning and the streetlights weren't all that bright."

Kat nodded tentatively. "Okay. So what?"

"So the defense attorney interviewed them prior to trial, and absolutely shredded them. Took them to task on the distance and the lighting and the beveled edges. By the time he was done, I didn't even believe them."

Kat smiled. "Perfect. So let's do that."

"No." Brunelle shook his head. "Not perfect. That was just an interview. Not under oath or anything, and certainly no jury. When the trial came, they were ready for him. They'd had a chance to think about everything. The light was dim, but the couple was right by a streetlight. They were a couple houses down, but they're thin houses so it wasn't that far. The beveled edges might distort things, but they weren't looking through the edges. And each of them said they'd had a chance to think about it since the interview and, after full and careful consideration, they were certain the defendant was guilty. The jury never saw the devastating cross the lawyer did in the interview. They only saw the completely ineffective cross he did at trial. And the jury convicted."

Kat frowned, but her expression betrayed her understanding.

Brunelle grinned. "We'll get our chance. But we need to keep our powder dry. If she made a mistake, let's get her to embrace it fully here, then expose it as a mistake on cross, in front of the jury."

Kat's frown gave way to a begrudging smile. "If I didn't know better, I'd think maybe you actually liked this defense gig."

Brunelle had to smile too. "It's growing on me."

Dr. Tuttle returned then, with Jim Westerly in tow. Brunelle stood and shook his hand, then commenced the introductions. "This is my investigator, Sophia Farinelli, and my, um…" He hesitated, not wanting to give Kat away, least of all her relationship with the defendant.

Kat stood up and shook Westerly's hand too. "Kat Anderson. I'm his partner."

Well, that's kind of true, Brunelle supposed. Misleading, but true. *She'd make a good lawyer.*

Westerly's expression betrayed a desire to inquire further, but there was something about the way Kat had said 'partner' that left the meaning ambiguous, and personal. Rather than ask anything, he said simply, "Nice to meet you."

They all sat down again and the interview could begin.

"Thank you for agreeing to meet with us," Sophia began. It wasn't like Tuttle really had a choice. The court rules required the prosecution to make its witnesses available for pre-trial interviews by the defense. Still, it was polite to thank her anyway. "We just have a few questions."

"Of course," Tuttle replied. "Glad to do it."

Good, thought Brunelle. *We're all lying.*

"I'd like to start with your conclusion," Sophia said. "Could you explain what you concluded regarding Vanessa Stephenson's death?"

"Did you read my written report?" Tuttle asked. It was a bitchy question. Of course they had. That wasn't the point. She needed to say it again, and explain it. She knew that. She was just being difficult.

"Pretend I haven't," Sophia replied. Brunelle smiled. It was the perfect reply.

Tuttle huffed and crossed her arms. Brunelle suppressed an even bigger smile. The jury was going to hate her.

"The cause of death was strangulation," Tuttle said simply.

"Okay, and strangulation causes asphyxiation," Sophia said. "How were you able to tell the difference between asphyxiation caused by strangulation and asphyxiation caused by the fire?"

Tuttle shifted in her seat. There was a certain lack of respect in the inquiry, questioning, however subtly, Tuttle's conclusion. But the answer was simple. "In strangulation, one sees injuries to the throat, which were present here. In addition, when someone dies from smoke inhalation, there is very visible blackening of the lung tissues, but that was totally absent here. She never breathed in any smoke, which tells me she was dead before the fire was set."

Brunelle nodded. That would have been his conclusion too. Westerly was going to have little difficulty convincing the jury the fire was set after Vanessa died.

But the real question was what happened before she died.

"Did you do a full external examination of Vanessa's body?" Sophia asked. She wasn't really looking at the doctor. Her eyes were cast down again at her notepad, checking off questions and writing down responses.

"Of course," Tuttle replied, but Brunelle saw Kat's almost imperceptible shake of her head. He met her eye and gave his own imperceptible shake of the head. His way of telling her to hush.

"Why?" Sophia asked.

Tuttle cocked her head then looked at Westerly, obviously confused by the question. "Why what?"

"Why," Sophia finally looked up, but her expression was still soft smiles, "did you do a full external examination of the body if it was so obvious it was a strangulation?"

Brunelle liked the question. He wondered if he'd like the response.

"Well, we always do an initial examination of the body," Tuttle began, a bit cautiously. "And we also photograph the body extensively, so we can always return to it later if needed."

Brunelle expected a bit more of an answer. She mostly avoided the question.

Sophia noticed it too. "So, perhaps the external examination wasn't as thorough as it would have been if there had been external trauma like stab or gunshot wounds, but you fully documented the condition of her body?"

Tuttle thought for a moment, looked to Westerly for confirmation, then nodded. "I think that's fair. There was no reason to believe there would be extensive external injuries. She was found dead inside a burned out store front. I checked for burns. Seeing there were none, my investigation turned next to likely smoke inhalation, but when I saw the lungs were pink, not black, that's when I discovered the fingerprint bruises on her neck."

"Could you tell the age of the bruises?"

Tuttle smiled, sensing a trick question apparently. "They were still purple. That's how I knew they were fresh. They hadn't had time to heal before she died."

Sophia ignored the smile. "What about the other bruises on her body? How old did they appear to be, based on healing?"

Tuttle's smile held, but it got just a touch shaky. "I don't recall any other bruising."

"You don't recall?" Sophia clarified, "Or you didn't look?"

Tuttle stiffened. "I told you, I always do a preliminary external examination, and I documented everything photographically. Any medical examiner could look at those photos and draw an accurate conclusion about bruising or any other external features."

And that's a wrap, thought Brunelle.

Apparently, Sophia agreed. She looked over to him. "I don't think I have any more questions. Do you, Mr. Brunelle?"

Brunelle shook his head. He just needed a transcript of Tuttle saying Kat's conclusions would be accurate. "No, I think we're good."

He knew not to ask Kat. She definitely had questions.

Brunelle stood up. The others followed suit. "Thank you for your time," he said. He turned to Westerly. "Thanks for setting this up."

"No problem," Westerly replied, "Who do you want to talk to next?"

Brunelle looked to Sophia. She looked to Westerly. "Detective Ayala," she said.

Westerly nodded. "Okay. I'll make that happen. Give me a

day or two. I don't know what his schedule is."

Then they parted company, Westerly staying back with Dr. Tuttle to debrief, and the defense team heading out into the hallway.

Kat was the first to speak. "Ooh, I wish you would have let me ask her some questions. What a shitty autopsy."

Brunelle smiled. He liked her enthusiasm. Well, he liked a lot more than that about her, but right then enthusiasm was toward the top of the list. And her eyes, the way they flashed when she was agitated.

"We'll get our chance," he soothed. "What about the bruising issue? I'd like to know if she had any bruises, especially on her arms. It might indicate a struggle if they were fresh. Can you examine the photos and give me your opinion?"

Kat shrugged. "I can examine them, but I can't give you a full opinion."

Brunelle raised an eyebrow. "Why not?"

"Garbage in, garbage out," Kat grumbled. "I can only examine what she bothered to photograph. I can't see an injury if she didn't photograph it."

"But she said she photographed everything," Sophia interjected.

"Not everything," Kat replied. "She was so ready to conclude strangulation, she didn't check for other injuries. The x-rays would have caught any broken bones, but there's a major area she didn't check but which is prone to receive injuries during a struggle."

"Where's that?" Brunelle asked.

"Her head," Kat answered. "She didn't shave her head, so she never checked for bruising to the back of her head. That would be huge in an alleged homicide."

"Are you saying someone hit her over the head?" Brunelle asked.

"No," Kat answered with a grin. "I can't say that. But she can't say it didn't happen."

Brunelle grinned too, enjoying for once the benefit of the reasonable doubt.

CHAPTER 23

The interview of Ayala would be different. For one thing, Kat wouldn't be there. She was back at the hotel, scouring over the autopsy photographs. Another difference was that while Tuttle was kind of a cold bitch, Ayala seemed like a pretty likeable guy. Brunelle kind of wished they weren't on opposite sides.

The final difference was that Brunelle would be asking the questions. Sophia would be taking notes and listening for inconsistencies with Ayala's written reports or any other aspect of the investigation.

"Thanks for meeting with us," Brunelle started once they were all seated around the conference table in the SFPD headquarters, again inside the Hall of Justice. Brunelle felt the urge to call someone 'Aquaman.'

Westerly was there again too. Ayala nodded toward the prosecutor. "Like I said, I got no problem talking with you, so long as Jim's present."

Brunelle nodded. He understood. That's how his cops played it too. Most of them were pleasant enough to the defense attorneys. They waited for them to leave the room before they bad-mouthed them.

"So how long have you been a detective?" Brunelle started. It was part ice-breaker—most men enjoyed talking about their careers— and part cross-exam prep. If he was a newbie detective, that would help Brunelle cast doubt on his work and conclusions.

"Twelve years," Ayala answered. "The last five in major crimes."

Nope. Not a newbie. Damn.

"Major crimes?" Brunelle followed up. "Not homicide?"

Ayala shook his head. "We don't have a homicide division. Just major crimes, but homicides are pretty major crimes, so I've done a lot of those. I just happened to be the one on call that night."

Brunelle nodded. "What about arson?"

Ayala shrugged. "I wouldn't say arson is really a major crime, I mean, it's important. All crimes are important, but…"

Brunelle gave a shake of his head. "No, I mean, have you ever done those? Like, before you went into major crimes?"

"Oh, right." Ayala thought for a moment. "We do have a couple of arson detectives, but I never did that. I had some cases that involved burned buildings, but they were secondary to some other, more violent crime. Kinda like here."

Brunelle liked that answer. He could expound on Ayala's lack of relevant experience in front of the jury. But not right then. Right then, he moved on.

"So, could you describe what you saw when you arrived?"

"The building was still smoking," Ayala explained, "but the fire was out. There were a lot of firefighters there and so I held the police back until the fire lieutenant okayed our entry. They'd called us when they found the body, so that was the first place we went."

Brunelle nodded. "Okay, describe the body."

This was key.

Ayala thought for a moment, then answered. "She was kinda curled up on her side in a back room. She almost looked peaceful. It seemed strange."

"Like someone posed her that way?" Westerly interjected.

"Right," Ayala agreed. "Like someone posed her."

Brunelle pursed his lips. Westerly shouldn't have done that. It was Brunelle's interview, not his. He could talk to Ayala any time he wanted by just picking up the phone. This was Brunelle's one shot. He knew all this because he'd sat in Westerly's chair more times than he could count. He had a policy: he never said anything. Anything. And he told the cop in advance. Sometimes, they expected help or even a little defense from him. But Brunelle didn't do that. Apart from potentially starting a time-consuming argument with the defense attorney, it was perfect fodder for cross.

And when I interviewed you on such-and-such date, isn't it true the prosecutor fed you answers to make my client look guilty?

So his conundrum was whether to tell Westerly to shut the hell up so he could get the information he needed from Ayala, or let him keep interrupting to use on cross-exam. But Westerly saw his hesitation and solved the dilemma.

"Sorry," he said. "I won't interrupt again."

Brunelle grinned and nodded. Perfect. He'd interrupted enough to bring it up on cross, and now he'd stay out of the way. Maybe. If he'd interrupted once, he might not be able to help himself later. Especially if Brunelle could piss him off a little bit. It was always nice to have a secondary goal.

He turned back to Ayala. "So you knew right away it was a homicide?"

Ayala shifted in his seat. "Uh, I wouldn't say that exactly. I mean, we came across a burned out building with a body inside. The initial thought was that she'd been overcome by the smoke."

Brunelle barely managed to suppress a smile.

"So we called the M.E.," Ayala continued, "to pick up the body. We didn't realize it was a homicide until the next day when Dr.

Tuttle called me."

"Did you attend the autopsy?" Brunelle asked. Detectives usually attended the autopsy on murder cases.

Ayala shook his head. "No. Like I said, we didn't know it was a homicide. We thought it was just an accident."

Brunelle considered how the investigation of the scene might have differed if they'd realized it was a homicide. Scene photography, evidence collection, arson investigation. All the stuff that either was missing from the reports entirely or seemed shoddy and hurried. Now he knew why, and was grateful for it. He also knew not to ask about it then.

"So, once you knew it was a murder." Brunelle moved on, "how did you identify a suspect?"

"Well, when it's an accident," Ayala replied, "there are no suspects, just family to notify. But when it's murder, well, you still start with the family."

Brunelle had to smile. "Why is that?"

Ayala shrugged. "Who can muster enough hatred to kill someone except someone who knows the person really well? Sure, gang murders and drive-bys can be pretty impersonal, but most murders are committed by someone the victim knows intimately. In this case, that's your client."

"The husband," Brunelle acknowledged.

"The second husband," Ayala emphasized. Then he corrected himself. "Well, she was the second wife, I guess. She hadn't been married before. But the middle-aged divorced guy who marries the blond aerobics instructor fifteen years younger than him and then gets into financial difficulty? Oh yeah, he's suspect number one."

Brunelle nodded, to encourage more information, but he wasn't willing to agree with the detective's assertion.

"Plus," Ayala added, "the patrol officer who notified him of the death said he reacted kind of weird when he heard the news. We notified him that night, before the autopsy, so he was told it was an accidental death in a fire. Instead of breaking down or crying, he asked if there were any witnesses."

Brunelle winced. "Any witnesses?"

Ouch.

"Yeah," Ayala laughed. "So when Dr. Tuttle said it was a homicide, he was the first person we contacted."

Brunelle had to nod. *Makes sense.* "What happened?"

"Well, we didn't get very far," Ayala admitted. "We met him at his office. We tried to be all smooth and not let on that it was a murder investigation, but we didn't want to lose any confession either, so we went ahead and Mirandized him. But as soon as we finished, he asked if he was a suspect? When we hesitated—because, after all, he was—he saw right through us. And why wouldn't he? He knew he was the murderer. He lawyered up and so we placed him under arrest."

"So you never questioned him?"

"Nope," Ayala confirmed. "Once a suspect invokes, we stop all questioning."

Brunelle nodded. That was the rule. He was just hoping his guy might have said something to a cop other than, 'Were there any witnesses?'

"Do you do anything further on the investigation?"

Ayala thought for a moment, then replied, "The usual. Collected reports from the patrol guys. Sent some stuff to the crime lab. Booked all the evidence. Then forwarded the case to the prosecutor."

He gave a nod to Westerly, who returned it, then said, "And we filed the charges."

"Yeah," Brunelle replied. "I knew that."

He looked to Sophia. "Anything else?"

She nodded. "You mentioned financial difficulties. What

evidence did you find of that?"

"We talked with his partner," Ayala answered. "Over-something."

"Overstreet," Brunelle interjected.

"Right, Overstreet," Ayala said with a nod. "He said Stephenson hadn't really been pulling his weight around the practice. Overstreet was bringing in over seventy percent of the income, but Stephenson still wanted to split it fifty-fifty. Overstreet was thinking about dissolving the partnership."

"He told you that?" Brunelle questioned. "That's funny. He didn't say anything about that to us when we talked to him."

Westerly chuckled. "You'd be surprised what people don't tell you now that you're a defense attorney. But they'll tell us everything. They like us."

Brunelle had to nod. Westerly was right. And it would be the same with the jurors. Just one more thing to overcome.

"Anything else?" Sophia asked.

"Well, the life insurance on her was pretty hefty," Ayala went on. "But the M.E. told the insurance company it was murder, so they refused to pay out. Stephenson was the beneficiary."

That reminded Brunelle of one more question. "Was the studio insured?"

Ayala nodded. "The landlord had casualty insurance, and the victim and her partner had a renter's policy."

"Was my client the beneficiary of that policy too?"

Westerly handled that question. "No, but I wish he had been. That would be the last nail in the coffin, so to speak."

"Why?" Sophia asked. Brunelle wondered too, but was glad he didn't have to admit his ignorance.

"That would have shown premeditation to commit both the fire and the murder," Westerly answered. "It would have shown that Stephenson expected to burn the building down and made efforts to profit financially from it. No, the life insurance was the motive. The renter's insurance they had was just payable to Vanessa and her business partner. Just in case there was ever a fire or an earthquake or something. That's not motive, that's just insurance."

Brunelle considered for a moment, then decided to be grateful Jeremy hadn't been stupid enough to take out that insurance too. Although he supposed it was more likely that Jeremy just hadn't thought of it.

"Thanks," he said, standing up. "I think we're done."

Westerly stood up too and shook his hand with a grin. "You sure are."

CHAPTER 24

"That was chump," Sophia complained as she and Brunelle stepped out of the Hall of Justice. She was blonde again that day, so Supergirl.

"What was?" Brunelle asked. He didn't have to shade his eyes as much as he'd expected. They'd been inside for a long time, but it was long enough that the sun was behind the tree tops.

"That 'You sure are' comment as we finished," Sophia said. She pulled on a very fashionable pair of sunglasses that somehow both hid half her face and made the rest of it seem even more beautiful. "I hope you win this just so I can see that arrogant ass have to eat that comment."

Brunelle shrugged and smiled slightly. "He seems like a decent enough guy."

"He's a prosecutor," Sophia snapped back. "They're all the same." Then she stopped and looked over at Brunelle, who had also stopped, an eyebrow raised at her comment.

She burst out laughing. That snort laugh. It was incongruous with her Jackie O. sunglasses, but was becoming increasingly endearing. "Except you, of course," she barely managed to say through more chuckling.

Brunelle just shook his head good-naturedly. It had been a long day and he was looking forward to relaxing that night. He and Kat hadn't figured out their plans yet, but they likely involved dinner and the beach. He could handle a little ribbing from his investigator.

They were walking back toward Sophia's office. It was a lot closer than Dombrowski's, and there was no particular need to bring Dombrowski in. But Brunelle did want to sit down with Sophia to discuss next steps. Trial was fast approaching and he could tell there was some aspect of the case that was still eluding him. He was managing to carry on some further light banter with Sophia while his mind replayed some of the seemingly more significant bits of information they'd learned that day.

Dr. Tuttle said Vanessa was dead before the fire was set.

Det. Ayala said it initially looked like it was an accident.

Jeremy asked if there were any witnesses.

It didn't add up. There was something missing. But he didn't have any more time to think about it just then. There was something else he'd forgotten about. Jeremy's loan sharks. But they hadn't forgotten about him.

"Hello, Mr. Brunelle," said the man who'd punched him the last time. He stepped out from a doorway just as Brunelle and Sophia were about to pass. Any effort to step around him was made pointless by the sudden appearance of his two henchman from the next doorway down. They stepped up behind their leader, effectively blocking the way. "And this must be your client's lovely ex-wife."

Brunelle felt the adrenaline dump into his bloodstream. He didn't really want to get punched again. He also found it disconcerting they knew his name. On the other hand, they didn't know everything. As much as he didn't want Sophia dragged into it, he was relieved that Kat had stayed back at the hotel to review the autopsy reports.

He didn't correct the thug. Neither did Sophia. She was smart.

Thug looked Sophia up and down brazenly the same way Brunelle had done surreptitiously. She was worth the up-and-down look. But it still bothered Brunelle. And distracted him, eager to defend her honor but smart enough not to challenge three likely-armed criminals.

"If this is about the money Stephenson borrowed from you," Brunelle said, "I don't know anything about that. I represent him on his criminal charges only."

Thug sneered at him and stepped into their space. "Don't patronize me. You represent him on everything he needs help on. And he needs help on this." He locked eyes with Brunelle. "*You* need help with this."

Brunelle knew there was no point in arguing. Not right then. He needed to figure out how to make these guys go away. That meant another meeting with Jeremy. And likely a loan from the Adonis corporate account, authorized by Overstreet. So in a way, Thug was right. He was going to end up representing Jeremy on this. He wondered absently if that might possibly be a crime. Accessory to usury?

His legal ruminations were interrupted by Thug. He had turned his attention to Sophia. "You get us that money, Mr. Brunelle. Or else something bad might happen. To you. Or..." He reached up suddenly and grabbed Sophia by the throat. "To someone you care about."

Sophia instinctively grabbed Thug's arm. Her nails dug into his skin, but he didn't loosen his grip. Brunelle made a halting movement in Thug's direction, but a gesture from one of the other men exposing the gun in his belt let him know not to try anything.

"Do we understand each other, Mr. Brunelle?" Thug asked without letting go of Sophia's neck.

Brunelle nodded stiffly. "Yes."

Thug let go of Sophia and she curled away, rubbing her throat.

She didn't cough, telling Brunelle it had been about control and fear, not actually hurting her.

"Good," the loan shark said. "Make arrangements. One week. We know where to find you."

With that, he turned his back to Brunelle and walked through the other two men, who kept their eyes on Brunelle to make sure he didn't try anything. Once their leader was safely past them, they too turned and the three of them disappeared down the next alleyway.

"Are you all right?" Brunelle reached out and touched Sophia's shoulders, but she shook off his hand.

"I'm fine," she said evenly, still rubbing the sides of her neck. "A little pissed, but fine."

"We need to talk to Jeremy," Brunelle said.

But Sophia shook her head. "No. We need to talk to Laura Mayer."

CHAPTER 25

"Remind me again," Brunelle said as they stepped into the elevator, "why we're bothering Laura Mayer instead of Gary Overstreet?"

"Because," Sophia replied, pressing the button, "we need to reorient her incentives."

Brunelle raised an eye to Kat, who had insisted on coming along—to give a human face to their business proposal—but she just shrugged. He looked back to his investigator. "How's that again?"

Sophia smiled. "She already has skin in the game," Sophia explained enigmatically. "We need to make sure she wins no matter who loses."

With that, the elevator doors opened again and they stepped into the hallway. "Besides," Sophia continued as they walked the short distance to Laura Mayer's condo, "Overstreet would say no, and then tell everyone. We need someone who will say yes, and be discrete about it."

They'd reached Laura's condo. Sophia raised a ringed and bangled hand.

Knock! Knock! Knock!

"Maybe we should have called first," Brunelle suggested.

"No," Sophia assured. "That would've given her a chance to figure out how to say no."

The door opened and a clearly surprised Laura Mayer greeted them.

"Well, hello, Mr. Brunelle, Ms. Farinelli," she managed to say upon seeing him. Then she quickly nodded to the other woman in the hallway. "I don't believe we've met."

Kat extended her hand. "Dr. Kat Anderson. I'm Jeremy's ex-wife."

Laura smiled tightly. "Very nice to finally meet you, Kat. I've heard a lot about you. Good things, all of them, I assure you. Please come in."

Kat didn't look particularly assured, but they stepped inside and again sat around the coffee table. This time, Laura hadn't been expecting them, so there wasn't any tea ready. She slipped into the kitchen to start a pot of coffee and returned to her guests.

"So tell me," she asked as she sat down on an upholstered loveseat, "to what do I owe this unexpected visit?"

Brunelle opened his mouth to start the pitch, but Kat jumped in first.

"We need your help," she said. Then, she admitted the truth. "Jeremy needs your help."

Laura nodded. But she also pursed her lips, crossed her arms, and sat back in her seat—none of which were under 'eager to help' in the body language dictionary.

"Not to be rude, darling," she finally said, the word 'darling' simply underscoring somehow that she was a bit older and a bit better off than any of them, "but why should I help the man who murdered my business partner?"

"Allegedly murdered," Brunelle corrected. He thought it the lawyerly thing to do. He forgot he wasn't supposed to be a lawyer just then.

"He didn't murder anyone," Kat spat at him. "He's innocent. Jesus, David, try to remember that."

Brunelle offered a contrite smile. "Right. Sorry."

"I'm afraid, dear," Laura interjected, "that none of us really know what happened that night. But the authorities seem convinced of his guilt, and I dare say none of us are unbiased."

Brunelle thought for a moment. "Sophia is."

That seemed to surprise even Sophia. "I'm part of the defense team," she said. "So I'm biased too."

But Brunelle shook his head. "No, that's not biased. That's just doing your job. Kat's his ex-wife. I'm Kat's, uh…"

Kat rolled her eyes. "Oh, for God's sake, David. Can't you even say 'boyfriend'?"

"Right," Brunelle grinned. "Boyfriend. That. And Laura, you were Vanessa's business partner and friend. But Sophia doesn't know anyone involved."

All eyes turned to the private investigator. After a moment she shrugged. "I suppose that's probably true. This is a case like any other. I care, but it's professional. For you all, it's personal."

Laura nodded. "All right then, Sophia. What do you think? Did Jeremy murder Vanessa?"

Sophia thought for several seconds, then shrugged again. This time a pretty little flinch of the shoulders. "I don't know. And again, I don't really care. It's kind of irrelevant."

Laura raised her eyebrows. "Irrelevant?"

Sophia nodded. "I've been hired to do a job. I'll do it, and extremely well too. Then I'll get hired to do the next job."

Laura and the others considered Sophia's answer for a moment.

"And anyway," Sophia continued, "we didn't come about that. We came to ask for money."

"Money?" Laura practically gasped. "You want me to pay for

Jeremy's defense?"

Brunelle wasn't sure this was how he would have handled it, but it was too late. He lowered his head into his hand, but Kat seized the opening.

"No," she said, "We want to borrow some money, temporarily, to pay off a loan Jeremy took out. From, well, from a loan shark."

Laura cocked her head, as if she were assessing just how insane these people in her home really were. "Is this some sort of sick joke?"

"No," Kat assured.

There was a long pause as Laura eyeballed her guests a bit more. "How much are we talking about?" she asked.

Kat looked to Brunelle who had raised his face again. "Twenty thousand," he said.

"Twenty thousand dollars?" Laura repeated. "And why in the hell would I do that?"

Kat reached out and exposed the red marks on Sophia's neck. "Because if you don't, they'll take it out on us." She looked over to Brunelle. "Show her your bruise too, David."

Brunelle hesitated then pointed to the yellowy spot on his cheek that marked where the bruise had mostly healed.

"They assaulted you?" Laura asked, aghast. "You're just his criminal lawyer."

"They didn't seem to care," Brunelle explained.

"And they thought Sophia was me," Kat added, letting Sophia's silky tresses drop back over her neck. "I don't want to think what they'll do when they hear my teenage daughter is in town for the trial."

That seemed to strike a chord with Laura. Up until the Lizzy comment she seemed shocked, but potentially unimpressed. But the thought of a teenage girl being victimized seemed to move her. "Even if I were willing to help, where do you suggest I get the money?"

"Your insurance settlement," Sophia answered immediately.

Laura raised an eyebrow. Gears turned behind her eyes. Brunelle guessed she was trying to decide whether to admit she'd received a settlement. "I need that money to recoup my losses."

Sophia didn't hesitate to reply. "You can double your money."

That got the affluent woman's attention. She uncrossed her arms. "How?"

"The payment to Vanessa is being held up by the criminal charges," Sophia explained, having discussed the matter with Brunelle and Kat on the way over, They had always drawn government checks and been on the county's malpractice insurance policy. Sophia the Entrepreneur was the expert on business, risks, and casualty insurance. "Once Jeremy is acquitted, he'll receive the payment through Vanessa's estate and he can repay you."

Laura narrowed her eyes. "That doesn't double my money."

Sophia smiled darkly. "And if he's convicted, they'll deny the claim as to Vanessa. You'll be the only beneficiary and you'll receive the entire settlement payment."

Brunelle's jaw dropped, but not nearly as far as Kat's.

"What are you doing?" Kat demanded. Her question was directed to Sophia, but she smacked Brunelle's arm. He was closer.

"It's a simple business proposition," Sophia explained. "Either way, Ms. Mayer wins. And we get the big uglies to go away."

Sophia turned back to Laura. "So what do you say?"

"I'm not convinced," she said. "What if I loan him the money, he's acquitted, and they still don't pay out? Then I'm out twenty thousand dollars. I need a guarantee the loan will be paid back."

"It will be," Brunelle jumped in. "Jeremy was borrowing from his practice without telling his partner. This is his loan, not ours. We're just the ones getting harassed. Maybe we can get him to agree to secure the loan with assets from his practice. But we don't want to go to a bank with this, for obvious reasons."

Laura pursed her lips again and tapped them thoughtfully. The pitch was over. She just needed to give her answer. The other three in the room waited for it. Finally she lowered her hand from her face and nodded. "I need to see the books for Jeremy's practice. If I'm going to loan money based on a security interest in a business, I need to know how solvent that business is. That kind of thing can be hidden pretty easily, but I'll be able to tell." She gestured toward her luxurious home. "I didn't get here not understanding how business works."

Brunelle figured that was all too true. "Done," he said. "We'll get you those A.S.A.P."

Sophia stood up and extended her hand, knowing to get going once the agreement had been made, lest it be rescinded upon a second thought. "Thank you, Ms. Mayer."

Laura seemed to appreciate the termination of their meeting. She stood up and shook Sophia's hand. "I'll look forward to seeing the books. Thank you for coming by."

The visitors quickly made their leave, Brunelle only slightly disappointed they hadn't gotten around to actually drinking any of the freshly brewed coffee. They waited until they were downstairs in the lobby again before anyone said anything,

"That went fairly well," Brunelle opined.

Kat had to agree. "Honestly, I thought she'd say no."

"She had to say yes," Sophia replied. "She thinks Jeremy's guilty and she has money riding on it. Now she knows we know that. So she had to agree to help—just to make it look like she had a reason for him to be acquitted too."

"She doesn't?" Kat asked, a bit dejected by Sophia's practicality.

"Her best case is still a conviction," Sophia replied. "She'll get her money from the insurance company. Plus a bonus."

"What bonus?" Brunelle asked.

"The guilty verdict," Sophia answered. "Remember, polite or not, she thinks Jeremy murdered her friend."

Kat frowned and looked away. Brunelle put a hand on her shoulder. She didn't respond, but she didn't shrug it off either. Brunelle decided to change the subject.

"So how do we get the Adonis books?' he asked. "We seem to be a pretty good team. Maybe we should all go visit Dr. Overstreet together and explain the circumstances."

But Sophia shook her head. "No, I don't think we want to do that. We don't want to arm him with that kind of information. He's the type who'd call the authorities."

Brunelle found that amusing. He used to be that type. Hell, he used to be the authorities. "Then how do we do it?" He asked.

Sophia smiled again, but it was that sultry smile she seemed able to call up like water from a well. "Leave it to me," she practically purred. "I can be very convincing."

Of that, Brunelle had no doubt.

And for the expression that apparently betrayed his thoughts, Kat gave him a sharp elbow in his ribs.

CHAPTER 26

Sophia was every bit as convincing as she'd claimed. She went to Adonis the next morning and was back at Kat and Brunelle's hotel by noon with a full set of the Adonis books, and more.

"How'd you manage that?" Brunelle was dense enough to ask.

Sophia cocked her head and put a hand on her hip, which accentuated both the bounce of her now-auburn curls and the pinch of her waist. "Really? Overstreet's a man."

"So am I," Brunelle replied.

"Right. So stop looking at her tits," Kat interrupted and took the paperwork from Sophia, "and start looking at the books."

Sophia surrendered another snort laugh and Brunelle could feel himself surrendering a blush.

"I wasn't looking at her tits," he whispered to Kat as Sophia went to fetch a pen from her purse.

"What were you looking at?" Kat whispered back with a crooked grin.

Brunelle hesitated. "Her eyes."

Kat shook her head. "That's a lie. And a stupid one. No woman wants her boyfriend looking in some other woman's eyes."

Brunelle knew it was a lie. He was looking at her hair, but that seemed like a worse answer. "What should I have said?"

Kat paused then answered, "You should have said you were looking at me."

"But I wasn't," Brunelle protested.

"You weren't looking at her eyes either."

Brunelle nodded, unsure what to say next. He guessed the right choice might be nothing.

"I don't care if you look at her eyes today," Kat finally said, "as long as it's my eyes you're looking into tonight."

Brunelle smiled, imagining what else their bodies would be doing as he gazed into her eyes. "Deal."

Sophia stepped back over to the smallish hotel room table they were using as a makeshift desk. Kat was spreading out the records and arranging them. Brunelle was trying to see what they said. Sophia picked up a file folder that had separate records in it. "These," she announced, a bit triumphantly, "are not records for Adonis. They're records for Inner Beauty Dance and Dreams."

"Vanessa's studio?" Brunelle asked. "How did you get those?"

"Vanessa *and Laura's* studio," Sophia corrected. "After I convinced Dr. Overstreet to let me take copies of the books, I also convinced him to just give me access to the file cabinet and take what I needed. These were tucked in the back of the bottom drawer."

Brunelle took the file folder and started thumbing through the papers within. "Do you think Jeremy had these to keep track of where the money was going? That's pretty careless to leave them where Overstreet could find them."

"Careless," Kat repeated. "Yep, that's Jeremy all right."

"A careless plastic surgeon?" Brunelle questioned. "That seems like a bad combination."

"Maybe that's why Overstreet was pulling in seventy percent of the income," Sophia said, examining a ledger. "No wonder he was thinking about splitting from Jeremy."

Kat came over and looked at the same ledger. Brunelle started delving into the books of Inner Dreams and Fantasies or whatever. It took a couple of hours, with lots of exchanged ledgers, countless figures scribbled on scrap paper, and one delivery pizza, but eventually they were able to tease out two very important things.

"So, Jeremy embezzled well over fifty thousand from Adonis," Brunelle said.

"And he was using Inner Beauty to launder it," Sophia concluded.

"But why?" Kat asked. She'd seemed able to convince herself her ex-husband wasn't a murderer, but the records made it nearly impossible to deny he was a thief.

"The real question is where," Brunelle said. "Where did the money go? Inner Beauty was bankrupt."

"Who had access to those accounts?" Kat asked.

"Vanessa," Sophia answered. "And Laura Mayer."

"But Vanessa is dead," Kat said, "and Laura just agreed to loan Jeremy twenty grand. Why would she do that if she was already taking the money he was embezzling?"

They all sat in thought for several moments.

"Because she doesn't want us to know she was stealing the money," Kat suggested.

"Because she and Jeremy were doing it together," Sophia added.

"Because Vanessa wasn't having an affair with Gary Overstreet," Brunelle realized. "Jeremy was having an affair with Laura Mayer."

CHAPTER 27

The plan was to divide and conquer. Actually, the plan was to divide and hope not to be conquered themselves. Sophia and Kat went to drop the books off with Laura, minus the ones for Inner Beauty Dance and Dreams. Sophia, because she was the investigator. Kat, because she insisted on doing *something*.

That something was not going to be what Brunelle was doing. Brunelle was going to see Jeremy again, and he didn't need Kat with him, throwing off the dynamic. Brunelle didn't really think Jeremy was fucking Laura Mayer. But he couldn't rule it out either. So he had some things he needed to say to his client, and he needed to keep control of the conversation. Somehow, staying in control was always difficult when Kat was involved.

Jeremy actually seemed glad to see him as he walked into the conference room. Brunelle supposed it had been a while since he'd stopped by. He knew inmates could get pretty bored on the inside, and started to look forward to attorney visits almost like it was family visiting hours. But it wasn't. This was business.

Jeremy greeted him and sat down on the other side of the glass, eager to hear what news his attorney had for him. Brunelle had lots of news, but had decided that most of it didn't need to be communicated just then. Embezzlement from Adonis. Adultery with Laura. Important topics, but also landmines. Only one was a crime, but both would make the jury hate him. More importantly, though, each was a motive, if Vanessa had found out.

Since Jeremy wasn't being honest with him anyway. Brunelle figured he'd rather figure it out himself than get sidetracked in another one of Jeremy's equivocations. So rather than broach those subjects just yet, Brunelle stuck to the most pressing issue.

"Laura Mayer is loaning you twenty thousand dollars," he said bluntly.

Just because he wasn't going to mention the affair explicitly didn't mean he couldn't have a little fun poking Jeremy and seeing how he reacted.

"Wha—?" he sputtered. "Laura? Twenty thousand dollars? Why? What the hell are you talking about?"

"I'm talking about three Russian guys and a loan that's gonna get me killed."

Jeremy's shocked expression softened. He blinked and looked down. "Oh."

"And not just me, Jeremy," Brunelle went on. "My investigator was with me this time. They thought she was Kat."

Jeremy jerked his gaze up again.

"They didn't treat her very nicely, Jeremy."

"What did they do?"

Brunelle frowned. "Not as much as they will next time. Especially if it's really Kat with me. You need to put this to bed. Better you owe Laura Mayer twenty-K than Vigo the Russian mobster."

Jeremy nodded. "Moldovan, actually."

"What?" Brunelle cocked his head.

"Moldovan," Jeremy repeated. "I don't think they're Russian. They're Moldovan."

"Where the fuck is Moldovia?" Brunelle asked.

"Moldova," Jeremy corrected with a shrug. "And I don't know exactly. Eastern Europe, I guess."

Brunelle shook the thought from his head. It really didn't matter where Moldova was. "Laura insisted on seeing the Adonis books though before she'd agree to lend you the money."

Jeremy's expression returned to that combination of surprise and panic.

"Don't sweat it, Jeremy," Brunelle interjected before his client could protest. "We already told her what you were doing with the books. She just wants to make sure she gets paid back."

"You told her?" Jeremy complained. "Isn't that attorney-client privilege or something?"

Brunelle hadn't thought of that. But he knew enough to deny it then. "No, I represent you on the criminal case. This is personal. They aren't related."

Jeremy didn't reply; he just looked away. So Brunelle followed up with, "Right?"

Jeremy looked back, but didn't quite make eye contact. "Right. Of course not."

Brunelle tapped his fingers on the small counter in front of him. He was still new to the whole defense gig, but he'd talked plenty with his friends on the other side. He'd always been impressed by the complexity of the attorney-criminal relationship, and grateful he didn't have to deal with it. Detectives told you the truth or pretty soon they weren't detectives any more. Same with patrol officers, and forensic scientists, and prosecutors for that matter. So he decided to try out one of the spiels he'd heard about from one of the defense attorneys he had some begrudging respect for.

"Okay, listen up, Jeremy. I'm going to say a few things and I don't want you to say anything back. Don't argue. Don't comment. Don't even agree. Nothing. Got it? Good.

"Because, see, here's the thing. As a defense attorney I can pull a lot of shit. I can sandbag the prosecution with late witnesses. I can withhold information that helps them and hurts us. But one thing I can't do is suborn perjury. I can't put a witness on the stand knowing they're going to lie. That's the one thing I can't do.

"So, shut up. I don't want to know the truth. If I know the truth and I know you're going to lie, I can't put you on the stand. But If I don't know the truth and I don't know what you're going to say, then I can put you on the stand and you can say whatever the hell you want. If it's a lie, that's on you. I didn't know you were going to lie, so I didn't suborn it."

He looked Jeremy in the eye. "Understood?"

Jeremy didn't reply, which meant he did.

"Good," Brunelle went on. "So I'm going to tell you some things I think might be going on. Things that would be really bad if they are going on. Things that give you a motive for murder if Vanessa found out about them. And when I say them, you shut up. You think about it, and I may ask you later, but right now, you don't say shit. Got it?"

Jeremy just stared at him. But he didn't argue either. *Good.*

"First of all, that money you were pulling out of Adonis, that's embezzlement. You can tell yourself you were a partner and you could do that, but Gary would disagree and so would a jury. You don't hide shit it's okay to do, and you hid it.

"Second, that money didn't go to support Vanessa's studio. I've looked at those books too, and if you'd given her as much money as you took out of Adonis, she would've been flush with cash, not bankrupt. Which means it was going to someplace, or *someone* else.

"Which brings me to my last point. I know Vanessa was a lot younger than you. And I know that young stuff can get old after a while, like eating candy at every meal. And I know that Laura Mayer is an older, attractive woman who probably satisfied your head as much as your dick. But if the prosecutor finds out you were having an affair with her, you are one hundred percent officially fucked. There's not a jury in California that wouldn't convict you. So if you need to do anything to wrap that up and make sure it goes away, then by all means, do it, but I don't want to hear about it."

Brunelle was done. Jeremy was shell-shocked. But he followed his lawyer's advice and didn't say anything.

"The status conference is next week," Brunelle said, standing up. "We'll talk again then. In the meantime, if you have any questions, don't ask them."

Jeremy stood up too. He nodded. "Thanks, Dave," he said, a bit unsteadily.

Brunelle surrendered a crooked smile. He nodded too. "Sure thing, Jeremy. We're all human. But that doesn't make us murderers. See you next week."

CHAPTER 28

As Brunelle stepped into the courtroom of San Francisco County Superior Court Judge Phyllis Carlisle, he was reminded of the old phrase: 'A good lawyer knows the law. A great lawyer knows the judge.'

Through more research than he usually liked, Brunelle had managed to learn at least some California law, but he definitely didn't know Judge Carlisle. He'd forgotten how nice it was to be assigned to a particular judge and knowing what that judge was like. Did he start early or late? Did she like a bit of humor to lighten the mood, or straight professionalism because of the seriousness of the matter? Did they go to law school together? What were his kids doing? How did she like her new boat? Was he thinking about retiring? Was she new and eager to prove she deserved the appointment from the governor?

Brunelle didn't know any of that about Carlisle. All he'd managed to glean was that he might be in for a bit of a struggle. When Dombrowski heard he'd been assigned to Carlisle for the trial, all he said was "Good luck with that," and cracked open another beer. Sophia wasn't much help either, claiming to be just the investigator. But Westerly's smile as he walked into the courtroom was enough to convince Brunelle he had an uphill battle ahead of him.

"Good morning, Dave," Westerly said as he rolled in with his trial briefcase, leather with an extendable handle. "Lovely day for a status conference, don't you think?"

It was a nice enough day. Better weather than up in Seattle, Brunelle guessed. Whether it was a good day for court, he didn't know yet. "Sure," he agreed anyway. "I'm looking forward to meeting our judge."

Westerly offered a wry smile. "Oh, that's right," he said. "You're not from around here."

Brunelle knew an opportunity when he saw it. "So tell me about Judge Carlisle. Do I have more to fear than fear itself?"

But Westerly shook his head. "Oh, no. You're going to have to figure this one out on your own. No help from the other team."

Brunelle fought off a frown. He was really looking forward to rejoining that team.

Then the secure door to the jail transport hallway clanked open and in walked the reason he'd been traded. Jeremy Stephenson, handcuffed, leg-chained, and escorted by two large, heavily armed corrections officers. Jeremy looked every bit the pencil-necked professional between their bulging forearms. Still, he managed a weak smile as he was led to the defense table and shook Brunelle's hand as best he could with the handcuffs still on. "Hey, Dave."

"Hey, Jeremy." They shook hands then sat down. Brunelle looked up at the nearest corrections officer. "Could you unhandcuff him for the hearing?"

The officer hesitated then looked to Westerly. The D.A. gave a nod and the corrections officer shrugged. "Okay, but he better not try anything."

Brunelle looked at his client. "You're right. He better not."

Jeremy looked hurt for a moment, but was pleasantly distracted as the guard removed his restraints. He rubbed his wrists as the officer stepped back with the handcuffs dangled from his grip.

"Thanks, Dave. So what's today's hearing for? Are we still going to trial next week?"

Brunelle nodded. "That's what today's hearing is for. To see if we're really going to trial next week."

"Are we?"

"Are you gonna take that manslaughter and arson offer?"

Jeremy shook his head. "No way."

Brunelle shrugged. "Then we're going to trial next week."

"All rise!" The bailiff had slipped in to announce the judge without Brunelle even seeing him. Brunelle jumped to his feet and pulled his client up with him. "The Superior Court for the County of San Francisco is now in session, the Honorable Phyllis Carlisle presiding."

Judge Carlisle emerged from her chambers and ascended the steps to her seat on the bench. Given what he'd heard, somehow Brunelle had pictured a tall scarecrow of a woman, with gray hair in an uncomfortable bun, a sharp nose between squinting eyes, and a frowning mouth. Instead, Judge Carlisle was very, very short—probably not even five feet tall, with untamed brown hair and noticeably large brown eyes. She looked like a robed owl perched on a branch above them.

"Be seated," she instructed, in a rather even tone, Brunelle thought. Everyone did, even the corrections officers—which Brunelle found a bit odd. The guards usually stayed standing back in his home court.

"Call the case, Mr. Prosecutor," Judge Carlisle ordered, "and introduce yourself for the record."

Westerly stood to address the court. At least that formality seemed to exist in both states. "This is the matter of the People of California versus Jeremy Stephenson," Westerly announced. "I am James Westerly, Assistant District Attorney on behalf of the people."

Brunelle allowed himself a twinge of jealously. In Seattle, he always represented 'the State.' He kind of liked the sound of representing 'the people.' Oh well. He stood to introduce himself and his client.

"May it please the court," he started formally, "I am David Brunelle, represe—"

"Order!" Carlisle screeched. "Order in my court!" She pointed an accusatory finger at Brunelle. "You will wait until you are addressed by this court, counselor. You will not speak out of turn." Then she banged her gavel. "I find you in contempt of this court."

Contempt of court?! Brunelle thought. He'd never, ever been held in contempt of court. You could get disbarred for that.

Before he could even gather his wits enough to figure out how to reply, Carlisle pronounced, "I hereby fine you the sum of one dollar, payable immediately to my bailiff."

Brunelle looked around the courtroom. Jeremy appeared appropriately dismayed at his lawyer having pissed off the judge. The corrections officers were trying to hide their grins, and Westerly just looked at him and nodded, then tipped his head toward the bailiff.

Brunelle was about to apologize, maybe even use it as a launching pad for trying to talk his way out of the contempt finding, but decided instead to pull out his wallet and extract a one dollar bill. He stepped around his table and over to the bailiff who took it with boredom. *This must happen a lot,* Brunelle deduced.

He returned to his position standing next to Jeremy and awaited further instructions. Carlisle eyed him for several seconds, her eyes even wider than normal. Brunelle knew what a crazy owl looked like.

Finally, she returned her eyelids to a normal position and raised her chin slightly to Brunelle. "Please introduce yourself and your client, counselor."

Brunelle looked over at Westerly again, unsure despite the invitation. Westerly again nodded, and so Brunelle looked up to face the wise old owl. "David Brunelle, Your Honor. I represent the defendant, Jeremy Stephenson."

Brunelle sat down again and eyed the judge warily as she smiled to herself, quite self-satisfied. "I would apologize, Mr. Brunelle," she said, "except that I have nothing for which to apologize. I am the judge and there are rules and I will enforce those rules."

Brunelle didn't really see a question or other invitation to respond in her statement so he simply nodded and waited.

"You will find," Carlisle went on, "that I am a fair judge, and a wise judge, and a good judge. But you will not find me to be an easy judge."

Again, not really a need to reply. Another nod. He stole a glance at Westerly, who was pretending to take notes about something.

"Is the defense ready for the status conference, Mr. Brunelle?"

Finally a question. And he knew the answer. "Yes, Your Honor."

Carlisle looked to Westerly. "Are the people ready, Mr. Westerly?"

The D.A. nodded. "Yes, Your Honor."

Carlisle nodded to herself several times. "Good, good, good," she muttered. Then she looked up sharply. "Let us begin."

Brunelle replied instinctively, "Yes, Yo—" but caught himself as the judge widened an avian eye at him.

He expected to be fined another dollar, but Carlisle relaxed her eye and spun her head to the prosecutor. "Charges?"

"Murder in the first degree," Westerly replied, "and arson in the first degree."

Judge Carlisle swiveled her head back to Brunelle. "Defenses?"

Brunelle grimaced. He wished he could have said 'alibi' or

'duress' or even 'entrapment.' But he had nothing. Not even the best one, 'self-defense.' Self-defense was only available after you admitted you did it. It was the 'Yes, I did it, but I *had* to' defense. The best part was that once you claimed self-defense, the prosecution had to disprove it, and beyond a reasonable doubt. No small task. But Jeremy had insisted he hadn't killed Vanessa. Which meant Brunelle couldn't claim self-defense. That left only one option.

"General denial," Brunelle answered. It was as lame as it sounded. The 'I'm not saying I didn't do it, I'm just saying you can't prove it' defense. The one the guilty people used.

Carlisle raised an eyebrow. "General denial," she repeated. "Are you certain?"

Brunelle frowned. He considered 'alibi', but sitting at home alone reading a book wasn't an alibi. It was a fucking lie. An alibi required a witness, and the most likely witness was the woman Jeremy was with. The one who just loaned Jeremy twenty thousand dollars. But she wasn't about to come forward and apparently Jeremy wasn't going to ask her to. "Yes, Your Honor. General denial."

And so it went. The Judge checking off the items on her checklist, first with Westerly then with Brunelle. Witness lists filed? Interviews completed? Jury questionnaires filed? Everything ready for trial?

"Yes, Your Honor," Westerly answered. "The people are ready for trial."

"Is the defendant ready for trial, Mr. Brunelle?"

Brunelle nodded, but more out of resignation than conviction. "Yes, Your Honor."

CHAPTER 29

Actually, Brunelle wasn't completely ready for trial. There was one more thing to do. One last conversation with Jeremy. The one the defense attorneys called the 'come to Jesus' talk.

Unfortunately, Kat had insisted on coming along. It was unfortunate for two reasons. First, it would definitely impinge on his tough guy defense attorney shtick. But more importantly, he'd avoided watching the two of them interact to that point. He wasn't looking forward to being the third wheel.

But when Kat wanted something, Kat usually got it. Brunelle had kind of given up resisting.

And now that she was 'on the defense team,' Kat could come with Brunelle to the jail even if it wasn't family visiting hours, which it wasn't. But that was just as well. Lizzy wasn't flying down until the night before the trial. Kat wasn't going to make her miss the trial, but she was going to minimize the amount of school she missed. One more fucking thing for Lizzy's mom and dad to talk about while lawyer-boyfriend counted the tiles on the ceiling.

"Kat!" Jeremy exclaimed as he stepped into his half of the consultation room. He actually stopped in the doorway, but the guard pushed him in and closed the door. He hesitated for a moment, then sat down reluctantly. He tried to smooth his hair and checked his shirt for stains. Obviously he didn't bother to clean up for Brunelle, but for his ex-wife—his first real love, most likely—he wanted to look as good as he could, regardless of the circumstances.

Brunelle would have felt bad for him, but he was too busy feeling glad that Jeremy hadn't shaved and couldn't quite get that one tuft of hair in the back to lay down.

"Hello, Jeremy," Kat said. Even her cold, businesslike voice had a certain warmth to it. Brunelle wasn't sure what Jeremy had done to lose her, but he knew two things: he was an idiot to have done it, and Brunelle was glad he did.

"What are you doing here?" Jeremy asked. "I mean, I'm glad to see you, but I—I don't understand."

"I'm helping David out," Kat replied, this time with an edge to her warmth. Like a blade heated in a fire. Doubly deadly. "And we need to talk."

Brunelle raised an eyebrow. She had told him she was just tagging along. She wanted to be part of the final consultation. She wanted to make sure everything was ready and Jeremy was as informed and as prepared as he could be.

She turned to Brunelle. "Could you step out for a minute, David?"

Brunelle's other eyebrow lifted. Apart from the fact that it was, technically, an attorney-client visit and not a family visit, he also didn't want to be completely excluded. It was one thing to be the third wheel. It was another to be the spare laying in the garage.

But he said, "Sure." Of course he did. It was Kat.

He stepped outside into the small hallway on the other side of the conference room door. He thought he'd count ceiling tiles, but instead he found himself contemplating the cinderblock wall, its pock-marked face only partially smoothed over by the layers of institutional gray paint spread across it over the years.

Everything had imperfections, some were just more obvious than others. And it was human nature to try to correct those imperfections. Or if they couldn't be corrected, then to conceal them, even temporarily. Jeremy Stephenson and Gary Overstreet had made careers of it, but they weren't the only ones. Laura Mayer's perfect luxury condo undoubtedly covered her own scars and failings. Westerly seemed put together, but that was only because Brunelle didn't really know him yet. And Judge Carlisle was obviously overcompensating for far more than Brunelle ever wanted to know. He stopped his analysis at himself, and Kat. He didn't need to dwell on his own imperfections. And as imperfect as he knew Kat was—she had to be, she was human—he enjoyed the feeling that even her flaws were perfect, parts of the immaculate whole. A part of him knew from experience that the illusion would fade, but the better part of him knew not to hurry the fading along.

He turned from the wall and gazed unfocused down the hallway. He kicked at the linoleum and wondered how late room service was open. He didn't think about the trial really; there'd be time and occasion to worry about that later. And he didn't think much about Lizzy's impending arrival. He didn't think about Duncan at all, and certainly not Yamata tearing up the place with what were supposed to be his cases. Mostly, he just shoved his hands in his pockets and waited for his girlfriend to be done talking to her ex-husband. It sucked.

But eventually, it was over.

Kat opened the door and stepped out to join him in the hallway. "Okay," she said. "We can go."

"Go?" Brunelle replied. "I haven't even talked to him."

Kat shook her head. "No need. I talked to him. We're done."

Brunelle looked at her for a moment, then opened the door to the room. But Jeremy was already gone, on his way back to his cell.

Brunelle turned back to Kat. "I thought I was in charge here?"

"You did?" Kat laughed. Then she stood on her toes and kissed his cheek. "Silly you."

CHAPTER 30

The night before trial found Brunelle leaning on his hotel balcony, watching the sun set and considering what was to come. Lizzy had arrived that morning. The three of them spent the day walking around the city ignoring the reason they were all there. After dinner they retired to the hotel room, where Lizzy could click on the TV and she and her mom could continue to whistle past her father's graveyard.

But Brunelle didn't want to watch TV. He had work to do. Or at least, work to think about.

"Penny for your thoughts." Kat put a hand on his back and slid in next to him at the balcony railing. "And no jokes about lawyers' thoughts being worth a hundred dollars an hour."

Brunelle smiled. He'd used that one before, but he wasn't really in the mood for it anyway. "Damn. That's my best joke. Guess I better think of something else."

Kat rubbed her hand across his back. "You could just answer my question. You look like you've got the weight of the world on your shoulders."

Brunelle laughed quietly, then turned back toward the hotel room. "Naw, just the weight of her world."

Kat turned too to see her daughter sprawled out on the bed, gazing at the TV, remote in one hand, diet cola in the other. She looked like she didn't have a care in the world. The grown-ups knew better.

"Don't put too much pressure on yourself, David," Kat said. They both turned back to watch the sky swelling pink and orange over the building tops. "Jeremy got himself into this, not you."

Brunelle shrugged. "Yeah, but it's my job to get him out of it."

Kat reached out and took his hand. "I know you'll do your best. That's all I can ask."

"What if my best isn't good enough?" Brunelle turned to her. "I'm not really a defense attorney."

"You're the best lawyer I know," Kat replied. "If anyone can get Jeremy out of this mess, you can."

Brunelle turned away again and shook his head. "I don't know, Kat. I don't have a lot to work with. They have motive, means, and opportunity. The only things I've been able to uncover are more motives." He frowned. "And it doesn't help that he keeps lying to me."

Kat nodded and put her arm around his waist. "I know."

Brunelle thought for a few seconds, mulling whether to ask the next question. Finally, without looking over to her, he said, "He didn't lie to you, did he?"

Kat chuckled. "He lied to me all the time. That's why we split up. That, and what he was lying about."

Brunelle smiled and put his own arm around her. "I meant when you talked to him at the jail. He didn't lie to you then, did he?"

Kat paused. "No," she finally said.

"What did he say?" Brunelle asked. He tried to sound only casually interested. But she knew him too well for that to work.

Kat shrugged. "Nothing, really."

Brunelle laughed. "Now who's lying?"

Kat laughed too. Then her expression turned serious again. "He said he's scared."

Brunelle nodded. "Yeah, that makes sense. He should be."

Kat laughed again. "Even his own lawyer says he should be scared. Yep, he's fucked."

Brunelle laughed lightly. But it was too serious a conversation for it to last. "Did you tell him the truth?"

Kat turned to look up at him. "About what?"

Brunelle shrugged. "I dunno. About his chances, maybe. Or…"

She took his chin in her hand and made him look at her. "Or what, David?"

Another shrug, but he didn't turn away. "Did you tell him you loved him? Is that why you wanted me to leave?"

Kat smiled. Her eyes sparkled from the setting sun. "I wanted you to leave so I could tell him how fucking lucky he is to have you as a lawyer. If you were there when I said it, he'd think I was saying it for your benefit, not his."

Brunelle smiled. "You avoided my real question," he observed.

Kat smiled too. "You're good. Jeremy's gonna be just fine."

Brunelle leaned forward and gave her a quick kiss. "You're still doing it."

Kat chuckled and kissed him back. Then she admitted, "Yes, when I left I told him I loved him. I do. But I'm not in love with him. We spent a lot of years together and we have a child in common. Of course I still love him."

Brunelle shrugged and tried to keep his smile. He was insightful enough to understand he didn't have the same life experience as Kat. "Of course," he agreed.

"But," Kat leaned up and kissed him again, not a quick peck either, "I adore you."

Brunelle's smile reached his eyes. He put his hands on Kat's hips and tipped his forehead against hers. "I adore you too."

Then the moment passed as they both remembered the teenage girl inside the hotel room. Brunelle turned to look at Lizzy, keeping his hands on his girlfriend's hips. "This really sucks," he said. "It's way more pressure than I realized. If I lose a case as a prosecutor, it doesn't feel good, but no one goes to prison. No one's *dad* goes to prison."

"Don't worry, David," Kat replied. "You'll do it."

Brunelle shrugged and looked back in her eyes. "What if I don't? What if he gets convicted and Lizzy loses her dad?"

But Kat shook her head. "No, I mean you're going to do your best, right?"

Brunelle surrendered a crooked grin. He looked again at Lizzy. "I sure am."

Kat hugged him. "Then you're going to do it. You're going to do your best. That's enough."

Brunelle hugged her back and rested his cheek on her head. He wished it were enough for him.

CHAPTER 31

In truth, doing his best wasn't enough. Brunelle didn't just want to do his best. He wanted to win. And not necessarily for the right reasons. Not just for those reasons, anyway. Not just for Lizzy and Kat and Jeremy and justice and the American flag and all that. He wanted to win because he wanted to win. He was used to winning. And a win would be one hell of a notch on his belt.

Prosecutors win most of their cases. Not because they're better than defense attorneys, but because all the cards are stacked in their favor. The defendant is supposed to be guilty. That is, prosecutors aren't supposed to be prosecuting innocent people. There's a reason the judge has to keep telling the jurors that the defendant is presumed innocent, that they can't hold it against him if he doesn't testify, and that cops are no more credible than other witness. The reason is that jurors—that ten percent of good citizens who actually show up for jury service instead of throwing away the summons—they believe in the system. They believe innocent people don't go to prison, cops aren't dirty, and if they were innocent they'd sure as hell take the stand and say so. So they listen to the judge, then go back into the jury room and vote to convict the guy who must have done something to get in trouble, based on the word of the cop who we have to be able to trust, and even if no one says it during deliberations, jeez, the defendant didn't even try to defend himself. Another guilty verdict. Another notch in the prosecutor's belt.

But this. To go to another state and win a murder case as a defense attorney? That would seal his reputation. Brunelle hadn't won all of his cases as a prosecutor, but he'd won most of them. If he could come back to Seattle as a victorious defense attorney too, well, it wouldn't matter one fuck what Yamata had done while he was gone. His legend would be complete.

And that's what was secretly going through his head as he walked into Judge Carlisle's courtroom the morning of trial to see Jim Westerly already setting out his law books and legal pad just as orderly and right-angled as Brunelle ever did.

"Morning, Jim," Brunelle greeted his opponent. No reason not to be civil.

"Morning, Dave," Westerly replied. "Ready to go?"

Brunelle nodded. "I guess so," he demurred. He didn't want to put Westerly on notice that he was bringing his A-game. Let him think Brunelle was only half-hearted, the prosecutor in him dulling his desire to gain the acquittal. "We'll see in a few minutes."

Before any more small talk could occur, the secure side door to the jail corridor clanked open and in walked Jeremy Stephenson, between two large and heavily armed guards. Jeremy was dressed in street clothes—a suit and tie Kat had brought from his apartment. Juries weren't supposed to know that a defendant was in custody. Another fiction to make it seem like everything was fair. He was presumed innocent after all, right? Just ignore the man behind the curtain—and the armed officers within lunging distance of the 'alleged' murderer.

Jeremy waited for the corrections officers to remove his wrist and ankle shackles, then shook Brunelle's hand. "Hey, Dave. Good to see you."

Brunelle could see how nervous Jeremy was. His face was pale and gaunt, his eyes a bit too wide, and his hand was so clammy it was almost dripping. Of all the people involved, Brunelle supposed, Jeremy had the most to lose. If the jury convicted him, he'd go to prison for the rest of his life. Everyone else would go home and eat dinner.

Brunelle guided Jeremy into his seat at counsel table then sat down next to him. He pulled a legal pad and a pen out of his briefcase and slid them over to his client.

"Here," Brunelle said. "This is yours. If you have a question, write it down, If you want to tell me something, write it down. If you have to go to the bathroom, write it down. I need to pay attention to everything that's being said. I can't do that if you're grabbing my arm and whispering in my ear. And besides, that kind of stuff looks shady. The jury won't like it. Just look like you're taking notes, as calm and confident as can be, After all, you're innocent, right?"

Jeremy hesitated as he processed Brunelle's verbal barrage. Then, a moment too late, he finally said, "Right. I'm innocent."

Brunelle sighed. "Work on that. You're going to testify. You better be more convincing than that."

Jeremy nodded weakly. "Okay." Then, "Really? I'm going to testify?"

"Did you do it?" Brunelle asked flatly.

"No," Jeremy insisted. "Of course not."

Brunelle nodded and started pulling his books and materials out of his briefcase and onto the table. "Then you damn well better tell the jury that."

Brunelle was about to expound on his theories about defendant's testifying and jury assumptions and what exactly does 'beyond a reasonable doubt' mean anyway, but he noticed Jeremy break eye contact and look over his shoulder toward the door to the hallway. He also noticed the look in Jeremy's eye.

Brunelle turned to see Lizzy walking into the courtroom, her mother right behind. They took a seat in the front row, the space reserved for the defendant's family. Lizzy raised her hand. "Hi, Daddy."

Jeremy waved back weakly. "Hey, Liz." But he didn't get to say more. The closest corrections officer smacked the back of his chair. "Eyes front," he commanded. "No interacting with the gallery."

A reminder to Jeremy of what he was facing for the rest of his life.

Jeremy looked askance to Brunelle, but Brunelle nodded in agreement. That was the rule. He needed his client to follow it. "Sorry, Jeremy." And he was. A little.

But Brunelle could turn around if he wanted to, and he did. A professional nod and controlled smile to his girlfriend, who offered the same back to him. He looked to Lizzy next, but she only managed a small and unconvincing grin.

Brunelle turned around again and tried to gather his thoughts before the judge took the bench. But that's exactly when she decided to. At the stroke of nine.

"All rise!" commanded the bailiff, and Judge Carlisle ascended to her perch above her onlookers.

"You may be seated," she announced after taking a moment to ensure that everyone had in fact risen.

She was a control freak and probably more than a little crazy, but her O.C.D. had proven its advantages. They had selected a jury in record time and Brunelle had no doubt the trial would go quickly. No lazy ten a.m. starts like some of the older, almost-retired judges he'd been in front of. They were going from nine to five with a one hour lunch and one fifteen minute break each half day—and only then because the court reporter's fingers would fall off otherwise.

So when the first day of trial started, the trial actually started. The bailiff led the jurors from the jury room to the jury box, the attorneys sat down at their tables, and Judge Carlisle announced, "Ladies and gentlemen, please give your attention to Mr. James Westerly, who will deliver the opening statement on behalf of the People."

CHAPTER 32

Westerly thanked the judge then rose and took his place standing before the jury. He steepled his hands thoughtfully and nodded to the jurors.

"This is a murder case," he started. "Jeremy Stephenson killed his wife. But he's not a monster."

Brunelle frowned. *Damn it.* Westerly was going the reasonable route. The same one Brunelle would have gone with. Opening statement was about promises. It was defined as a statement of what the lawyer believed the evidence would show. A promise of sorts. And the worst thing a lawyer could do in opening was overpromise.

"Jeremy Stephenson is a doctor, a businessman, and a father. And he was a husband. But he started to make decisions that didn't work out for him. And ultimately he made a decision that didn't work out for his wife, Vanessa Stephenson. Vanessa is dead because of the decisions that Jeremy Stephenson made. And he needs to be held responsible for those decisions."

Westerly lowered his hands but didn't move from his spot rooted directly in front of the jury. He was a seasoned trial attorney. Pacing was distracting. He could afford to just stand there. He had the jury's attention. He had everyone's attention. He was the D.A. in a murder case.

"I'm going to tell you a little bit about Dr. Stephenson. Then I'm going to tell you a little bit about Vanessa Stephenson. Then I'm going to tell you about some of the problems they were having. And then finally I'm going to tell you what happened on the night Vanessa died, and you'll understand why Dr. Stephenson is charged with murder in the first degree."

Brunelle had to hand it to Westerly. Lawyers weren't allowed to argue guilt in opening statement. That would be 'argumentative' and an objection would be sustained. Openings were supposed to simply state what the lawyer expected the evidence to show. Westerly was walking right up to the line without crossing it. Brunelle decided to pay even better attention, not just so he could respond properly with his own opening, but also to see if he could pick up some pointers.

"Jeremy Stephenson is a physician," Westerly went on, elevating Jeremy even more by calling him a 'physician' rather than simple 'doctor.' "In fact, he's a surgeon. A cosmetic surgeon. He went to four years of college, then four years of medical school, then more schooling for his specialty, followed by long years of residency at several different hospitals. He studied hard and worked long hours to get where he is today professionally.

"Dr. Stephenson is also a father. Vanessa was his second wife. They didn't have any children together, but he has a teenage daughter from his first marriage who lives up in Seattle, Washington. And although they live apart, Dr. Stephenson remained involved in her upbringing."

Brunelle tried not to shake his head. He was prepared to counter Westerly's arguments about what happened the night Vanessa died. He didn't expect to have to call bullshit on a glowing description of his client. Jeremy had been about as involved in Lizzy's upbringing as a random stranger on the street. But Brunelle was unlikely to tell the jury that. Let them think he was a better father than he really was. Lizzy was in the front row after all. They might actually buy it.

"And until the night of Vanessa's death, Dr. Stephenson appeared to be a loving and doting husband. He bankrolled her business, a dance studio Vanessa had always wanted to own. They went on vacations and did all the things a happy couple was supposed to do."

Westerly finally moved again. He raised a single hand and pointed to the jury. "But appearances can be deceiving."

Westerly lowered his hands and took two steps to his right, closer to the judge. It reinforced his position as the prosecutor, seeker of justice, agent of order, representative of the People. It also gave a chance for a dramatic pause after his last statement. And he could remind the jurors to keep their eyes on him, even if he moved. They did. He had them. They wanted to know the dirt. We all want to know the dirt.

"All was not well in his medical practice. And all was not well at home. Dr. Stephenson wasn't a solo practitioner. He had a partner, Gary Overstreet. The thing about partnerships is that all the money goes into one pot, then the partners take out equally. That works out fine if both partners are putting in about half, but things weren't going so well for Dr. Stephenson. He had fewer and fewer clients, and was bringing in less and less money. That can happen, but it wasn't just a dry spell. Dr. Overstreet is going to tell you that Dr. Stephenson wasn't pulling his weight. He was still a good surgeon, but he was neglecting his practice. He was distracted. By Vanessa. And her dance studio."

Westerly nodded and took one step back toward his original position. He was going to be talking about the victim. Getting back to the center of the jury would suggest reconnection with the jurors. Jurors didn't know about all these non-verbal aspects of trying a case.

Good trial attorneys did. And Jim Westerly, much to Brunelle's consternation, was a good trial attorney.

"The dance studio had always been a dream of Vanessa's. But dreams can't pay the bills, and the arts are a hard way to make a living. Vanessa loved the studio, and Dr. Stephenson loved Vanessa, so he started borrowing money from his medical practice to keep the studio afloat. The only problem was, he didn't tell Dr. Overstreet."

Brunelle nodded slightly. That was a problem. Although it was hardly the only one.

"At first, I'm sure Dr. Stephenson thought he'd be able to pay it back. At first, maybe he did. But Vanessa's studio needed more and more money. But no matter how much he borrowed, the studio needed more. He kept trying, but it wasn't working. And then the worst possible thing happened. The worst thing for Vanessa. She stopped being thankful."

Jeremy grabbed Brunelle's arm finally. Clearly, he took exception to Westerly's accusation. But Brunelle shrugged off his client's grasp and tapped the legal pad he'd given him. He needed to listen to Westerly, not Jeremy.

"Then the night came when Vanessa died. When Dr. Stephenson killed her. We may never know exactly what words were said that night, but we know this: words were exchanged, Jeremy choked his wife to death, then he set the studio on fire to cover his crime. Dr. Sylvia Tuttle, the medical examiner who performed the autopsy on Vanessa, will tell you that Vanessa was strangled to death, Dr. Stephenson's fingerprints left bruises on her neck. And Dr. Tuttle will also tell you that Vanessa's lungs had no smoke in them at all, meaning she had stopped breathing before the fire was set."

Brunelle suppressed a grin. Westerly's description of the actual murder was noticeably short on detail. That made sense. Jeremy had lawyered up and Vanessa couldn't speak from the grave. Still, it gave Brunelle an opening.

"So ladies and gentleman," Westerly began summing up, "you will hear from many witnesses, but there's one witness you won't hear from. Vanessa Stephenson. But the evidence will speak for her. The evidence will show that her husband, Jeremy Stephenson, lost his temper, and as a result, she lost her life. And at the end of this trial I will stand up again and ask you to return a verdict of guilty. Thank you."

Westerly nodded to the jurors then turned and retook his seat at the prosecutor's table.

It was a perfectly adequate opening statement. But it wasn't great. It lacked details, but more importantly, it lacked passion. Westerly was smart, but maybe not smart enough to show he cared.

Brunelle wouldn't make the same mistake.

"Ladies and gentleman," Judge Carlisle announced, "now please give your attention to Mr. Brunelle, who will deliver the opening statement of the defendant."

CHAPTER 33

Brunelle stood and nodded to the judge and Westerly. Then he took the same spot before the jury where Westerly had stood. Westerly had started by saying Jeremy wasn't a monster. The temptation was to repeat that. But Brunelle had learned a few things over the years. When Richard Nixon said he wasn't a crook, people knew that's exactly what he was. And when that Senate candidate from Delaware said she wasn't a witch, the one word everyone remembered was 'witch.' So Brunelle wasn't going to say Jeremy wasn't a monster. He wasn't going to say what Jeremy wasn't he was going to say what Jeremy was.

"Jeremy Stephenson is a doctor, a businessman, a father," Brunelle repeated Westerly, then paused just a beat before adding, "and a widower."

'Widower.' A strange thing to call a murderer. The jurors shook off their 'oh God, another lawyer is going to talk at us' expressions and most of them looked over at Jeremy to see if maybe, just maybe, he was real human being after all.

"The love of his life, Vanessa Stephenson, died tragically in a fire that also consumed her dream, a dance studio she and Jeremy had worked hard to build from the ground up. Vanessa went to the studio that night to attend to things—the way anyone does who's lucky enough to do work she loves. Jeremy stayed home, reading a book, relaxing from his own job, and waiting for his wife to come home to him. But instead of returning home, she died in a fire, and Jeremy's world was turned upside down. Not only did he lose his wife—his soul mate—he was suddenly arrested for her murder and sits here now before you, like Alice in Wonderland, trying to understand how he got here, an innocent man, accused of killing the woman he loved."

"Objection." Westerly stood up. "Argumentative."

It was argumentative, Brunelle knew. He had called his client innocent. How dare he? He looked up to Judge Carlisle, but didn't argue the objection.

"Sustained," Carlisle ruled. "You will refrain from further argument, Mr. Brunelle, and restrict yourself to a recitation of what you expect the evidence will show."

Brunelle nodded. "Yes, Your Honor." He didn't need to be held in contempt again, and certainly not in front of the jury. And besides, he'd gotten Westerly to object. The jury might not remember much of his opening, but they'd remember that the prosecutor didn't like it when Brunelle painted the picture of Jeremy sitting in the Queen of Hearts' court, no more guilty than a sweet young girl fallen into a rabbit hole.

"As I was saying," Brunelle turned back to the jurors, "Jeremy was at home that night. Alone. Reading a book. He doesn't have a dozen friends he was hanging out with that night who will come in and swear about his whereabouts that night. That's not how he spends his time. He's a surgeon, a businessman, a father, and a husband. He doesn't have time for much else. He doesn't live his life like he's going to need an alibi."

The weakness to Brunelle's case, of course, is that his client didn't have an alibi. He very well could have been at the studio that night, strangled Vanessa to death, and burned her studio down in an attempt to cover it all up. Brunelle only had Jeremy's word to say otherwise. And juries are naturally suspicious of a defendant's testimony. A defendant has every reason to lie, they figure. And they're right. But rather than argue with the jurors that they shouldn't think that way, rather than try to shame them for not really presuming his client innocent, Brunelle embraced that prejudice, then used it against them. The reason jurors believed defendants must have done something to be charged, is because the thought if an innocent person being charged with a crime is frightening. Make the jury feel that themselves, and they'll be terrified it could happen to them too.

"And so when Jeremy's quiet evening of reading and relaxing was finally interrupted, it wasn't by the return of his lovely bride, but by the banging on his door of a police officer. When Jeremy answered the door, he learned his wife was dead. Now, keep in mind, the authorities didn't think it was a murder yet. He simply learned that his wife died in a fire. An accident. At her studio, the one she'd always dreamed of, the one he'd taken great risks to finance and support."

Brunelle couldn't really deny that part of Westerly's opening, but he could shade it in positive terms. And move on quickly.

"It wasn't until the next day that the police and the medical examiner suddenly decided it was a murder. So they arrested Jeremy, for no reason other than he was the husband, and therefore the most likely, or at least the easiest, suspect."

"Objection." Again Westerly stood up at his place at counsel table. "This is also argument."

Brunelle turned to look up at Judge Carlisle. "I expect the evidence to support what I just told the jury."

Carlisle hesitated. That alone was a victory. Juries notice little things like that. "You're getting close, Mr. Brunelle. I will overrule this objection, but stay away from any further argument."

"Yes, Your Honor." Brunelle was smiling inside, but kept his features somber as he turned back to the jurors. Westerly's objections had punctuated his two most important points—innocent client, easy suspect—and Carlisle had validated the last one. Time to wrap up.

"The evidence will show that there were no witnesses to the death, the scene investigation was woefully inadequate, and the conclusions of the medical examiner little more than rank speculation. Dr. Jeremy Stephenson didn't murder his wife. He sits here accused of a crime he didn't commit, no more responsible for Vanessa's death than any of you. Thank you."

That last bit warranted another objection—probably several— but Brunelle sat down before Westerly could stand up again.

It had been short on details, but that was consistent with someone who had no idea what happened because he was home alone reading a book. It was a defense opening perhaps not worthy of Jessica Edwards, but Brunelle was pleased enough. Westerly looked stoic, and at least a few of the jurors looked worried. He had a fighting chance.

Carlisle interrupted his thoughts. "That concludes opening statements," she told the jury. Then she peered down at the prosecutor. "Mr. Westerly, you may call your first witness."

Westerly stood up. "The People call Dr. Gary Overstreet."

CHAPTER 34

Overstreet walked into the courtroom, head down and hands in his pockets. He didn't glance at Kat or Lizzy as he passed them in the gallery, and he certainly didn't look at Jeremy as he strode up to the witness stand. He looked every bit the successful California doctor: blue blazer over open-collared shirt, khakis, and shined shoes which suggested something nautical without being actual 'boat shoes.' He just needed a white captain's hat to hide that bald dome of his, Brunelle thought. The bailiff swore Overstreet in and he sat down quickly, locking his eyes on Westerly who took a position toward the back of the jury box.

"Good morning, sir," Westerly started.

Overstreet nodded in reply, but didn't say anything.

"Could you state your name for the record?" Westerly prompted.

"Gary Overstreet," he replied. He was visibly nervous, his voice taut and his breathing quick.

"How are you employed, Mr. Overstreet?" It was one of those stupid lawyer questions. Everyone knew he was a plastic surgeon and Jeremy's partner, but he had to say it out loud. It wasn't enough for the lawyers to say it—or anything—facts had to be stated by witnesses. So every witness examination usually started with questions everybody already knew the answers to. Brunelle had done it hundreds of times himself. It was only then that he noticed how irritating it was to listen to.

"I'm a physician," Overstreet answered. He kept his eyes glued to Westerly, lest they stray to the defendant's table. "A surgeon. A cosmetic and reconstructive surgeon."

"A plastic surgeon?" Westerly translated with a wry grin. It was important for the jury to understand. It was also important to make Overstreet seem honest. Giving haughty labels to what he did wouldn't help.

Still, Overstreet winced at the label. "That's an outdated term. I perform reconstructive surgery for medical and cosmetic reasons."

Westerly nodded. No need to fight that battle any more. "And are you in private practice?"

Overstreet thought for a moment, as he considered how to answer the question. "Yes," he finally said.

"By yourself?" Westerly prompted.

Overstreet again hesitated, but then shook his head. "No. I have a partner."

It was like pulling teeth. Brunelle usually preferred to take notes and appear mildly disinterested in the other side's case, but Overstreet's verbal foot-dragging was intriguing even him.

"Who's your partner, Dr. Overstreet?"

Overstreet finally acknowledged the man in the defendant's chair. He nodded toward the defense table and frowned. "Jeremy Stephenson."

Jeremy was scrawling furiously on his legal pad. He looked up long enough to acknowledge his name, but looked down again. Brunelle didn't like it. It seemed shady somehow.

Westerly continued his direct exam, in his even, professional tone. "How long have you been partners with Dr. Stephenson?"

Overstreet thought for a moment. "Almost five years."

"What's the name of your practice?" Westerly asked. "Is it Stephenson and Overstreet, or something like that?"

Westerly knew damn well what it was, but again, it was about getting the witness to tell the jury.

"No," Overstreet responded. "It's called Adonis Image Studio."

Westerly allowed himself a smile. "Quite the name."

Overstreet shrugged. "It's part of the marketing."

Westerly nodded. "Of course. In fact, let's talk a little bit about the business side of your practice."

Smooth transition, Brunelle had to admit to himself.

"Okay." Overstreet nodded back, but his expression went a little bit slack with trepidation.

"How is the business structured?"

"It's a professional services corporation," Overstreet replied.

Westerly needed to translate again. "Is that like a regular corporation? Did you issue stock? Is there a board of directors?"

"Oh, no, no," Overstreet waved off those suggestions. "No, the State of California requires doctors and lawyers to form professional services corporations instead of partnerships. It has to do with malpractice and taxation issues. No, it's basically a partnership. The IRS treats it like a partnership, and that's what really matters."

There were a couple of chuckles from the jury. Brunelle didn't mind. It wasn't like Overstreet was a cop. He was Jeremy's friend and partner. If the jury liked him, that was fine.

"Okay," Westerly replied. "And were there just the two partners, you and Dr. Stephenson?"

"Yes," Overstreet confirmed.

"And how were the profits disbursed?" Westerly asked. "Was it based on how much business you each brought in that year or that quarter or something?"

Overstreet shook his head. "No. We thought about doing that, but cosmetic surgery is a pretty unpredictable business. It's not like G.I.—that is, gastro-intestinal. If you do G.I., or urology, or ear-nose-and-throat, you always have customers. Er, patients, I mean. There are always people with stomach and bowel problems, urinary tract infections and enlarged prostates, sinus infections and throat cancer. That stuff happens, and those patients need doctors. Cosmetic surgery is different. Basically, all of our patients are seeking elective surgeries so we have to be far more business savvy than your average physician."

Brunelle found the answer a bit unappealing. He wondered if any of the jurors did too. As if feeling it too, Westerly tried to rehabilitate his overly business-minded witness.

"Well, some reconstructive surgeons also do more necessary surgeries, isn't that right?" he asked. "Like helping women who've been the victims of domestic violence, or fixing cleft palates in the Third World?"

Overstreet nodded. "Well, yes, some do."

"Do you?" Westerly hoped.

Overstreet shifted in his seat. "Uh, no. No, I don't." Then, perhaps to remind people who the real villain was, Overstreet looked at his partner. "But neither did Jeremy."

Great, Brunelle mentally rolled his eyes. He considered objecting to any further questions along those lines, but he felt pretty confident Westerly wanted to move along too.

"So if you and Dr. Stephenson didn't pay yourselves based on the amount you each took in, how did you pay yourselves?"

Overstreet nodded, then frowned slightly, showing he knew the import of the question. "It was fifty-fifty. We trusted each other." The frown deepened and he shrugged. "I trusted him."

"Did you later come to learn that your trust might have been misplaced?"

Overstreet hesitated, but admitted, "Yes."

"And how so?" Westerly was polite, but not so much that he wasn't going to extract what he needed.

Overstreet glanced at Jeremy, then looked to Westerly. "I recently learned Jeremy had been taking money out of our corporate account without telling me."

Several of the jurors nodded. They'd heard that much from Westerly in his opening.

"Do you know what he was taking the money out for?"

Brunelle stiffened a bit as an objection flashed through his mind. He could have stood up and said, 'Objection. Calls for speculation.' Carlisle would have granted it. Overstreet didn't really know what Jeremy had taken the money for. But Brunelle let the possible objection fade away. He hated objecting—it telegraphed pain to the jury. And besides, he really didn't mind if the jury heard the answer.

"I believe it was to help his wife," Overstreet responded.

Brunelle smiled. That was a good answer.

Westerly shifted his weight, obviously considering how to follow up the 'husband of the year' type of response Overstreet had just given. "But you don't know the exact details, right? Because he hid it from you?"

Overstreet nodded. "Right. It's just what I've heard since."

The logical next question was, 'Who did you hear that from?' but Westerly's problem was that Overstreet had likely heard it from him or his detectives, which made it hearsay. So instead, Westerly circled back to the main reason for calling Overstreet in the first place.

"So, you never gave Dr. Stephenson permission to drain your joint corporate account, correct?"

"Correct," Overstreet confirmed.

"And if you'd found out about it, what would you have done?"

Overstreet sat back and sighed. He thought for several seconds. "I'm not sure. Things weren't going all that well anyway. I was bringing in most of the clients any more. Jeremy was very distracted. I thought it was by his wife and her dance studio. I guess it was the money too. But I was already wondering whether I might do better on my own. If I'd found out about this, I think I probably would have left the partnership."

"And that might actually have improved your financial situation, correct?" Westerly asked.

Overstreet agreed. "I think so, yes."

"And," Westerly drove the point home, "it would have greatly damaged Dr. Stephenson's?"

Again, rank speculation, but Brunelle resisted the objection. Even if it were sustained, everyone would know the answer. No reason to highlight it by objecting.

"Yes," Overstreet answered. "I believe so."

Westerly nodded and looked up to the judge. "No further questions, Your Honor."

Carlisle turned her gaze to Brunelle. "Any cross examination, counsel?"

Brunelle stood up. "Yes, Your Honor. Thank you."

Brunelle's usual questioning spot was where Westerly had stood: right next to the jury box, farthest away from the witness. It made sure the witness kept his or her voice up—if Brunelle couldn't hear, nether could the jurors next to him—and also helped the witness look toward the jury when answering, which was always helpful to the jurors, and thereby to his case.

But cross was different. The jury still needed to be able to hear, but there was a certain drama in cross examination. Jurors expected a little confrontation, some word trickery, raised voices, or the top prize: a blurted out confession. Brunelle knew that kind of stuff never really happened, but that didn't mean the jurors weren't kind of hoping for it. Especially after a careful, and slightly boring, direct examination by the button-down prosecutor.

So Brunelle took a spot at the bar—the ledge that ran in front of the witness box, the bailiff, and the court reporter. It was where attorneys usually stood to address the court on motions and other matters that didn't require a jury. It enabled Brunelle to get close to Overstreet without being right on top of him. He was going to challenge Overstreet to give him what he wanted, but he wasn't going to browbeat a confession out of him or anything.

"Good morning, Dr. Overstreet," he began.

Overstreet offered a tentative smile. "Good morning."

"I just have a few questions," Brunelle said. He wanted Overstreet to relax a bit, but more importantly he wanted the jury to know two things: he wouldn't waste their time, and they should pay attention. Just a few questions suggested those few questions would be important.

"You and Dr. Stephenson were partners, correct?"

Overstreet nodded. "Correct." He'd already said as much.

"And isn't it true that partners each own one hundred percent of the partnership's assets?"

Overstreet narrowed his eyes and cocked his head at Brunelle. "I'm not sure I understand what you mean."

"I mean," Brunelle clarified, "that you and Dr. Stephenson didn't have any agreement that for every dollar that came in, fifty cents would go into your private account and fifty cents would go into his. All assets were held by the partnership, and you each had access to all of the funds."

Overstreet pursed his lips. "I guess so. I mean, that's not really how we treated it. It came in however it came in, and then we drew down from the account in equal shares."

Brunelle nodded. "I understand that, but as one of the partners, Dr. Stephenson had access to all of the money in the partnership account, correct?"

Overstreet shrugged. "I suppose so."

"So, when he withdrew money from that account, it wasn't theft, was it?"

"Theft?" Overstreet repeated. "Well, I kind of think so. I mean—"

Brunelle raised his hand. "I don't mean how it *felt* to you. I mean, technically, under the partnership agreement and the laws of the State of California, it wasn't actually theft, was it?"

Overstreet exhaled audibly and frowned. "No, I guess not."

It was an interesting subject. Brunelle knew more than one private attorney who'd been a partnership only to come to work Monday to find the accounts emptied. Perfectly legal, even if perfectly immoral. They said you had to be as careful selecting a business partner as selecting a spouse—maybe more so. Doctors probably didn't do that to each other as often as lawyers, but it served his purposes for cross. Time to move into a different area, but subtly, so the witness wouldn't see what was coming.

"But, setting aside this lapse of judgment in order to help his wife, Jeremy was a pretty good business partner, wasn't he?"

Overstreet thought for several seconds. Enough to cast doubt on his appraisal of Jeremy as a partner, but eventually he answered, "Yes. Jeremy was a good partner. Until all this."

Good enough, Brunelle decided. He'd take what concessions he could get.

"And in fact, you considered Dr. Stephenson a friend, correct?"

Overstreet nodded and looked over at Jeremy who had finally stopped scrawling on the pad. "Yes. And despite everything, I still do."

That was a nice touch, Brunelle thought. He pressed on. "And he's a pretty good doctor too, isn't he?"

Overstreet looked back to Brunelle. "One of the best cosmetic surgeons I know. That's why I was willing to be partners with him."

Brunelle nodded. He'd gotten almost everything he wanted. Just one more thing and he could sit down. He ticked off the list on his fingers.

"Good doctor, good partner, good friend. And you said he risked all of that by taking money to support his wife's dance studio. He risked his professional license, his professional reputation, and his friendship with you, all so he could do anything he could to prop up his wife's dream of owning a dance studio, isn't that right?'

Overstreet nodded. "That's right."

"Well, I'd say that would make him a pretty good husband, too, wouldn't it?"

"Objection!" Westerly stood up at counsel table. "Calls for speculation."

Carlisle looked to Brunelle. "Any response to the objection?"

Brunelle suppressed a smile. It didn't matter what Overstreet answered. He'd made his point, and Westerly's objection had made it into an exclamation point. Still, it didn't hurt to try to underline it. "It's opinion, Your Honor, not speculation. The witness should be allowed to answer, if he can."

Carlisle considered for a moment. "I'm going to sustain the objection," she ruled. "Do you have any further questions?"

Brunelle shook his head. "No, Your Honor. Thank you."

He sat down, and Overstreet was excused. Then Brunelle realized he should actually be glad for the objection. Overstreet could have said something damaging like, 'Yeah, until he killed her.' He'd broken the old lawyer rule, 'Never ask a question you don't already know the answer to.' Luckily, Overstreet was a doctor, not a professional witness. Brunelle would need to be more careful with the next witness.

Westerly stood up. "The People call Detective Frank Ayala."

CHAPTER 35

Ayala was dressed similarly to Overstreet, better in fact: khakis, suit coat, plus a tie. But somehow, he looked less put-together than the good doctor. The difference between someone who cared about looks versus someone who cared about results. Detectives were about results. Even if those results turned out to be wrong.

"Please tell the jury your name and occupation," Westerly began the direct exam from his same spot next to the jury box.

"Frank Ayala," the detective replied. "I'm a detective sergeant with the San Francisco Police Department."

"How long have you been with SFPD?"

"It'll be twenty years next spring," Ayala replied. He knew to deliver his answer to the jurors directly, rather than Westerly, and turned slightly to impress them with his decades of experience.

"Are you assigned to any particular department?"

Ayala nodded and again turned to the jury. "I'm in the major crimes unit. I've been a detective for twelve years, the last five in major crimes."

"Is there a homicide unit?" Westerly was barely able to even appear interested. This was all background stuff that he of course already knew. But the jury needed to hear it, so he'd trudge through the introductions. Brunelle listened keenly to see if it varied any from when they'd first met. It didn't. *Good*, he thought.

"No," Ayala answered. "Homicides are wrapped up into major crimes. I investigate all types of major crimes, including murders."

The perfect segue for Westerly. "And did you investigate a murder that occurred at the Inner Beauty dance studio?"

"Inner Beauty Dance and Dreams," Ayala corrected. "Yes, I was the lead detective on that investigation."

Brunelle considered objecting to Westerly's use of the word 'murder.' Whether it was murder or not was the jury's call. Murder was an *unlawful* killing. But the alternative to objecting was explaining, which was often better. He could make his point on cross examination.

"Please tell the jury," Westerly encouraged, "how you came to be involved in that investigation."

Ayala nodded again and looked to the jurors. "The original call was just for a fire in the SOMA district. A couple of patrol officers went to assist with crowd control, but it was a fire department scene. At least until the fire was under control and they could go inside. That's when they found the body."

"And that's when you were called in?" Westerly asked.

"Yes," Ayala confirmed.

"Because it was a murder?" Westerly pressed, even though he knew the answer.

"Uh, no," Ayala admitted. "People die in fires all the time. Well, not all the time, but it happens. Usually though, it's an accident, not murder. Still, the patrol guys find a body, they're gonna call a detective."

"When did it become apparent this was more than just a person who died accidentally in a fire?"

Ayala's comfortable demeanor slipped a bit. He shifted in his seat. "Not until the next morning, actually," he admitted. "The folks from the medical examiner collected the body that night. I got a call halfway through the autopsy from Dr. Tuttle."

Westerly interrupted just enough to orient the jury. "Who's Dr. Tuttle?"

"Dr. Tuttle is the medical examiner," Ayala told the jury. "She was performing the autopsy when she noticed something suspicious. A couple of things actually. So she called for a detective and it was my case."

"Thank you," Westerly interjected. "So what did Dr. Tuttle find suspicious?"

Again an objection flashed through Brunelle's mind. 'Calls for hearsay.' Ordinarily one witness can't tell the jury what another witness told him. Westerly should have to call Dr. Tuttle to testify about what she found suspicious. But Brunelle had two problems: first, Dr. Tuttle would undoubtedly be testifying, so no real point to objecting, and second, as long as Westerly could tie it to why the detective took whatever steps he took next, the judge would overrule the objection. It had a non-hearsay use, that it, it didn't really matter if it was truly suspicious, as long as it impacted Ayala's next steps. So Brunelle sat on his hands again. He was beginning to fully appreciate how frustrating being a defense attorney could really be.

"There were two things," Ayala replied. He ticked off fingers to the jury. "First, there were bruises on her throat. Second, there was no blackening to the interior of her lungs."

"And what did that suggest to Dr. Tuttle?" Westerly asked.

Ayala nodded and turned somberly to the jurors. "It was murder."

Brunelle rolled his eyes mentally. *Very dramatic. Bravo.*

"So what did you do with this information?" Westerly confirmed Brunelle's hearsay objection would have been overruled.

"The first thing I did was return to the scene," Ayala said.

"The second thing I did was contact Dr. Stephenson."

"Why did you go to the scene first?" Westerly asked.

"Well, before I contact a suspect," Ayala explained to the jurors, "I want to have as much information as possible. If it was murder, then the fire was probably deliberately set. Arson. To try to cover up the murder. I wanted to see if there was any evidence of that."

"And was there?"

"Yes. It was fairly obvious. Pretty amateur, actually. Someone used an accelerant—like gasoline or lighter fluid—and sprayed it on the walls every ten feet or so. There were scorch marks leading from the floor straight up to the main burn damage which was a few feet off the ground. Fire burns up, so the scorch lines told me there had been some flammable fluid poured down the walls."

"Then what did you do?"

"As I said," Ayala confirmed, "I went to speak to Dr. Stephenson."

Westerly folded his arms across his chest and raised one hand to his chin. "Now, did you speak to any other officers before you contacted Dr. Stephenson?"

Ayala nodded. "Yes."

"Why?"

Again a turn to the jury. "Dr. Stephenson had been informed the night before by some patrol officers that his wife had died in a fire. I wanted to see what reaction he'd had when he was told."

"And what reaction did he have?"

Again a possible hearsay objection, but again Westerly had set it up so it had a non-hearsay use: how it impacted the detective's subsequent steps.

"They said he didn't really show any emotion," Ayala answered. "And the only thing he asked was, 'Were there any witnesses?'"

"'Were there any witnesses?" Westerly confirmed. Not because he hadn't heard it, or didn't know damn well that was exactly what Ayala was going to say. He just wanted the jury to hear it more than once.

"Yes, sir," Ayala answered. "Were there any witnesses?"

Brunelle suppressed a wince. That really did hurt. He glanced at his client, but Jeremy was busy scrawling on his legal pad. Poor guy. He was a nervous wreck. But then again, Brunelle supposed, he probably should be. He was on trial for murder.

Westerly nodded for several seconds, letting the words really sink in for the jury. "So, did you contact Dr. Stephenson?"

"Yes. I called him at work and he agreed to come to the station," Ayala explained.

"Why would he do that?" Westerly questioned.

After all, Brunelle knew the suggestion, *he's a murderer.*

"The other option I gave him was that I come to his office." Ayala smiled to the jury. A few smiled back. *Damn it.* "I find the threat of the police coming to someone's work usually is enough to get them to come to the station."

"So what happened when Dr. Stephenson arrived at the station?"

Brunelle looked up, trying to mask his sudden spike of interest. This was a dangerous area for Westerly. What happened was Jeremy lawyered up and got arrested. But they couldn't tell the jury Jeremy refused to answer questions. That would be a comment on his right to remain silent. Grounds for a mistrial, and maybe even a dismissal if Brunelle could convince the judge they'd done it on purpose—unlikely, Brunelle knew, but he could hope.

Westerly's problem was that something as brief as 'We arrested him,' might look like the cops jumped to conclusions, but failure to mention the arrest would leave out the logical progression of the investigation. Brunelle raised a hand to his chin and waited for

Ayala's response, expecting he would like it either way.

"We introduced ourselves," Ayala started slowly. Brunelle wondered if Ayala had gotten the 'don't mention him invoking his right to remain silent' memo. But he supposed twenty years on the force had probably taught Ayala not to testify about that. "I explained that the autopsy had revealed his wife had been murdered."

Westerly shifted his weight. He wasn't supposed to lead the witness. He was supposed to ask open-ended questions. But another, 'What happened next?' might encourage Ayala to say something he shouldn't.

"And was Dr. Stephenson eventually placed under arrest for the murder of his wife?" Westerly gave in and led him. Even if Brunelle objected and the objection was sustained, Ayala would know what to say next. So Brunelle didn't bother.

Ayala got it. "Yes, sir."

"Thank you, detective." Westerly breathed a sigh of relief. "No further questions."

Carlisle looked to Brunelle. "Cross examination?"

Brunelle smiled as he stood up. "Yes, Your Honor."

This would be brief too, but no need to say that every time. The jury knew to pay attention now. He took the same spot at the bar. If he needed to be slightly confrontational with Jeremy's business partner, it was absolutely necessary with the lead detective.

"You've been a police officer for a very long time, haven't you?"

Ayala nodded and smiled to the jury. "Yes."

"You've done lots of different kinds of cases and interacted with different kinds of people, correct?"

Another nod. "Oh, yes."

"And different people react differently to similar situations, right? How one person reacts to their car being stolen might be very different than the next, for example, right?"

Ayala's nod was a little bit more begrudging this time. "Yes," he admitted. "I think that's generally true."

Ayala wasn't stupid. He knew where Brunelle was going. And Brunelle knew he knew. He just didn't care.

"I imagine you've responded to a lot of violent crimes, too, correct? Are people's reactions always the same at, say, a domestic violence call?"

Ayala twisted his mouth a bit. "Not exactly the same, but there are patterns people fall into."

Brunelle smiled. Ayala wasn't going to give it up without a fight. Good.

"Right," he said. "Some victims are glad you've come to help, others are angry you're there. Some cooperate and tell you what happened, others recant and say nothing happened, even when they've got a black eye and blood running out of their nose, right?'

Ayala hesitated, but nodded. Brunelle had nailed it. "Yes, that's true."

"And you never know which of those reactions you're going to get until you arrive and start talking to people, right?"

Again a moment's hesitation, but then the admission. "Right."

"There's no right way to react, is there?" Brunelle pressed. "Everyone's different, aren't they?"

Ayala frowned slightly, but agreed, "Yes, everyone's different."

Brunelle could smell the smallest amount of blood in the water. "So, what's the right way to react when someone tells you your wife is dead?"

Ayala hesitated, which was perfect, since Brunelle really didn't want him to answer that question. It was too open-ended. Cross exam was all about leading the witness. That was the first rule of cross: lead, lead, lead. So he jumped into the breach and rephrased the question. "You can't say my client's reaction wasn't within the normal range for someone who'd just been told his wife was dead, can you?"

"Well…" Ayala seemed ready to say just that.

So again, Brunelle rephrased. Or rather redirected. His question alone had made his point. Time to make another. "In fact, you weren't even there when he was told, were you? You just heard about it later, from a patrol officer who might not have anywhere near your experience, isn't that right?"

Westerly stood up. "I'm going to object, Your Honor. Counsel keeps asking compound questions."

Carlisle nodded like an owl bobble-head. "Objection sustained." She didn't even ask Brunelle for a response. "One question at a time, counselor."

Brunelle nodded to the judge. The objection was well taken. "You weren't actually there when my client was told his wife was dead, were you?'

Ayala sat up straight. "No, sir."

"Thank you." Brunelle nodded. Point made. Time to move on. "You did the fire investigation yourself, is that correct?"

Ayala pondered for a moment. "I wouldn't call it a fire investigation exactly. I investigated the crime scene and saw evidence of arson."

"But you've never been an arson investigator, have you?" Brunelle remembered their interview weeks earlier. He knew Ayala did too.

Ayala surrendered a small grin. "No, sir. That's correct. But I've seen plenty of fires."

Brunelle nodded affably. "Of course you have. And you've seen plenty of dead bodies. Do you perform the autopsies?"

Ayala's grin faded a bit. "No, sir."

"And you've carried a firearm for twenty years or more," Brunelle went on. "Fired tens of thousands of rounds at the firing range, I'm sure. Do you examine bullets and casings for ballistics comparisons?"

Ayala crossed his arms. The smile was gone. "No, sir. The crime lab guys do that."

"Have you ever worked a case with fingerprint evidence?"

"Yes, sir."

"Did you do the fingerprint comparison yourself?"

"No, sir."

"Have you ever collected DNA from a suspect?"

"Yes, sir."

"Did you do the DNA analysis yourself?"

"No, sir."

Brunelle could have gone on, but he knew when to stop. "But in this investigation—this *murder* investigation—you felt qualified to do the fire investigation yourself, is that right?"

Ayala uncrossed his arms and finally remembered to talk to the jury again. "I inspected the scene. When I did that, I saw obvious scorching from the use of an accelerant. I don't need to examine the gun to know when somebody's been shot, and I didn't need a fire investigator to tell me that fire had been deliberately set."

Brunelle actually believed Ayala, but it didn't matter. Not when he had a job to do. "Could you tell when it was set?"

Ayala cocked his head. "When?"

"Yes, when," Brunelle repeated. "Was it set before or after Vanessa died?"

Ayala's brow knitted together. "Dr. Tuttle concluded it was set after she died."

"So that conclusion was based on the autopsy," Brunelle clarified, "not your fire investigation?"

Ayala considered a moment longer, just to be certain, then answered. "That's correct."

Brunelle nodded. "Thank you. No further questions."

As he sat down, Jeremy broke the legal pad rule and whispered, "What does that have to do with anything?"

Brunelle just smiled. If Jeremy was wondering, then so was the jury.

CHAPTER 36

After Ayala, Westerly called a parade of lesser witnesses. Officers and firefighters and evidence technicians. Jeremy's question to the police began to seem prophetic: there were no witnesses. Not really. No one saw the fire start or Vanessa die. It was all collecting evidence afterward, taking statements, writing reports, blah blah blah. Necessary for the investigation, but boring for the jury. Still, Westerly had to call the witnesses necessary to prove his case. And he knew to finish strong.

"The People call Dr. Sylvia Tuttle."

The small-framed medical examiner flitted into the courtroom, clad in a well-tailored brown suit, and quickly took her seat on the witness stand. She was a sparrow to Carlisle's owl.

Westerly started with the usual: name, rank, serial number, and medical degrees. Tuttle had been with the medical examiner's office for X years, she'd done over X-thousand autopsies, she went to X medical school, and did her residency at X hospital. Then it was time to get to the important stuff: the autopsy.

"Did you perform an autopsy in this case, doctor?" Westerly asked.

"Yes," Tuttle replied with a confident nod. "I performed an

autopsy on Vanessa Stephenson."

"And afterward," Westerly stepped over to his counsel table and picked up a multi-page document, "did you write an autopsy report regarding your findings?"

Tuttle nodded again. "Yes, I did."

"Would it help your recollection if you could refer to your report while testifying?"

"It might," Tuttle replied. "I do a lot of autopsies. I did four that day, if I recall correctly."

Westerly handed Tuttle the report, which he'd previously had marked as an exhibit by the bailiff. Tuttle identified it as her autopsy report and Westerly moved on to the details.

"What did you determine was the manner of death in this case?"

Tuttle raised her chin slightly. "The manner of death was homicide."

Brunelle noticed she was delivering her answers to Westerly, not the jury, which suited him just fine. Still, he found it curious. She'd undoubtedly testified enough times to know she should turn to the jurors when answering questions. Maybe, Brunelle let himself hope, she was a bit uncomfortable in her conclusions.

"How did you reach that determination?" Westerly asked.

"It was a combination of several factors," Tuttle replied. "The external examination, the internal examination, and the circumstances under which the body was found."

Brunelle liked that answer. It gave him room to push her around on cross.

"Let's start with the external examination," Westerly said. "What did you observe that helped you conclude this was a homicide?"

"There was bruising to the throat," Tuttle answered. "Specifically, fingerprint bruises."

"And what are fingerprint bruises?" Westerly asked wisely. There might well be someone on the jury who would think that meant the killer actually left his fingerprints behind.

"Fingerprint bruises are bruises that are the size and shape of fingerprints," Tuttle explained. "They don't actually leave behind fingerprints, but they are made by pressure from fingers. It tells me that she was strangled manually and not with some sort of ligature, which would have left a long, thin bruise around the entire neck."

Brunelle recalled that Tuttle hadn't actually noticed those bruises until she opened up the lungs. Another fertile area for cross. Recalling that Kat had been there for that interview, he turned back quickly to glance at her, wondering what she thought of Tuttle's testimony.

Kat and Lizzy had spent every minute of the trial sitting in the front row, right behind Jeremy. It was important that the jury knew the defendant had family who cared about him. Up to that point, Kat had been there just for moral support—Jeremy's and Brunelle's. But this was different. Brunelle didn't care how she was feeling about the father of her daughter being tried for murder—well, not just that anyway. He cared what she thought about Tuttle's testimony professionally.

But Kat wasn't looking at him, or even at Jeremy. She was leaning forward, her chin on her fist, staring intently at her colleague on the stand.

Brunelle smiled to himself at her professional intensity, and turned back around. He needed to pay attention to the witness too.

"What did you discover," Westerly asked, "during the internal examination that helped you determine it was a homicide?"

Tuttle finally turned to the jurors. "When I cut open her lungs, they were perfectly pink inside." Something she was sure of, Brunelle noted.

"And why was that significant?"

"Because when someone dies of smoke inhalation," Tuttle explained to the jury, "the inside of their lungs are blackened."

"And that wasn't the case here?"

"No."

"So what does that mean?"

"It means," Tuttle announced, "that she was dead before the fire started."

Westerly took a moment to nod and pretend to gather his thoughts. Brunelle knew he wanted that bit of logic and conclusion to sink in with the jury before he moved on.

"So if the manner of death was homicide," he finally asked, "what was the *cause* of death?"

"The cause of death was strangulation."

"And how do you know that?"

"The combination of bruising on her throat and the fact that she wasn't breathing during the fire," Tuttle explained. "And there was no other indication of any other cause of death such as blunt or sharp force trauma."

"So no other injures?" Westerly translated.

"Correct."

"Just to her throat?"

"Correct."

"And so based on your autopsy and your review of relevant law enforcement reports, what is your expert opinion as to exactly how Vanessa Stephenson died?"

Tuttle sat up straight in her chair, but returned to delivering her answer to Westerly, not the jurors. "Vanessa Stephenson was strangled to death."

Westerly allowed a small grin. He was all but done. He'd finished direct exam of his final witness. It was like a pitcher walking into the dugout after striking out the side. "No further questions."

Westerly strode over to his counsel table as Brunelle stood up behind his.

"Any cross examination, Mr. Brunelle?" Carlisle asked.

But before Brunelle could answer, Kat jumped up and whispered, "David! David!"

Brunelle turned to see Kat leaning over the half-wall that separated the gallery from the courtroom's well. "David!"

Brunelle looked up at Carlisle and over at Westerly. Carlisle looked surprised, Westerly bemused.

"What is it?" he whispered to Kat.

"Just ask her one question," Kat whispered. "Ask her what room the body was found in."

"Uh, okay," Brunelle replied. "I can ask that."

"No, just that," Kat clarified. "Just that question, then sit down."

Brunelle just stared at her for a moment. He had an entire cross examination prepared. She was ripe for cross examination. There was so much there to play with. He shook his head. "No, I have to ask her more than that. I have to draw out the weaknesses in her testimony."

"Mr. Brunelle?" Carlisle interrupted, the irritation clear in her tone. "Are you going to conduct any cross examination?"

Kat reached out and grabbed Brunelle's hand. "Trust me, David. Just that one question. She won't know. Then sit down."

Another shake of his head. "Kat…"

"Please, David," Kat pleaded. "Trust me."

He just stared at her for a moment.

"Mr. Brunelle?" It was his last warning. One more time and he'd be in contempt again. And this time he knew it would be a lot more than one dollar.

Kat didn't say, 'Trust me' again. But her eyes held the thought.

Brunelle turned around. "Thank you, Your Honor. My apologies." He glanced at Westerly, whose bemusement had morphed into the slightest unease. Then he nodded to the witness. "I just have one question."

He could sense Kat relax behind him and she retook her seat as Brunelle approached the witness stand.

"What room was Vanessa's body found in?"

Tuttle cocked her head. "Excuse me?" As if she hadn't heard the question.

"I said, what room in the dance studio was Vanessa's body found in?" Brunelle repeated. "You don't know, do you?"

Tuttle looked down at her autopsy report, then back up at Brunelle. "Well, it's not in my actual autopsy report," she admitted. "But I'm sure it's in the police reports. Or the report of our techs who collected the body."

"But you don't know right now," Brunelle confirmed, "as you sit here and tell the jury your opinion that Vanessa was murdered, correct?"

Tuttle looked again at her report, then to Westerly, but she wasn't going to get any help from either. "No," she finally admitted. "I don't recall that right now."

Brunelle nodded. Then, despite his better instincts, he looked up to Judge Carlisle. "No further questions."

As he walked back to counsel table, mentally shaking his head at the missed opportunity to cross Tuttle fully, he was barely aware of Carlisle asking Westerly if he had any further questions, and Westerly gladly replying no, thus ending the examination of his last witness, and thus his case-in-chief.

"The People rest their case," Westerly announced as Brunelle sat down.

Carlisle banged her gavel. There were still a couple of hours left in the workday, but it was customary to let the defense start their case fresh the following morning. "Ladies and gentlemen," she announced to the jurors, "that concludes the People's case. We will adjourn until tomorrow morning, at which time the defendant will present his case."

Another bang of the gavel and the bailiff rose to escort the jurors out of the courtroom. Everyone else stood up too. The judge disappeared into her chambers, Westerly threw Brunelle a quizzical glance, and the gallery began their own mumbled conversations. Kat stepped up and took Brunelle's hand again.

"Thank you," she said.

But Brunelle just shook his head. "You've got some explaining to do, young lady."

CHAPTER 37

"She wasn't in the main studio," Kat explained over dinner at the steak restaurant across the street from the courthouse. "She was in the back. In the dressing room."

"So what?' Brunelle asked. He took a drink of his beer. Lizzy just sipped from her Coke, her eyes shifting between her mom and her mom's boyfriend.

"So that would also explain why her lungs weren't blackened," Kat replied. "I bet there was a lot less smoke damage in the back."

Brunelle shrugged. "Maybe. I'll have to check the reports to see where the fire allegedly started. But I don't see why that matters so much."

Kat set her wine glass down a little too hard. "Because Tuttle said she was dead before the fire was set based on her perfectly pink lungs. This is an alternate explanation."

"Again, so what?" Brunelle demanded. "She's still dead. And I don't think Jeremy dumped her body there after the fire was raging."

Kat's eyes flared and she leaned back in her chair, crossing her arms. Lizzy took a long, loud slurp through her straw.

"Jeremy didn't dump her body anywhere, David," Kat

growled. "He didn't kill her, remember? Or did you forget that?"

Brunelle narrowed his eyes. "I didn't forget anything. I can't forget something I don't know. I have no idea if he killed her."

Kat's arms dropped. "You think he killed her?"

Lizzy looked at him too, but not accusingly. More like desperately.

"I didn't say that," Brunelle insisted. "I said I don't know. I wasn't there. And he's been lying to me since I first introduced myself. So, no, I don't know if he did. Maybe he did. But I don't really care either. It's not about whether he killed her, it's about whether the State can prove it beyond a reasonable doubt. My job is to keep them from doing that."

Kat frowned but didn't immediately reply. Lizzy kept her eyes glued on him. He saw it out of the corner of his eyes, but kept his gaze locked on Kat.

"And my job is a lot easier if I can cross examine the witnesses against him," Brunelle went on. "Especially the goddamn medical examiner who conducted the autopsy."

Kat narrowed her own eyes and leaned forward onto the table. "Well, I'm sorry Mr. Lawyer-man. But quite honestly, you don't seem to be doing that great a job. Everybody thinks Jeremy did it— including you, apparently—and you haven't done anything to change that."

He slapped his hand on the table. "And I did even less when I only asked the medical examiner one fucking question."

Brunelle's slip in dropping an F-bomb succeeded in jarring the adults' attention to the teenager in their company. It wasn't as if Lizzy had never said it herself, they knew, but still. Poor form.

"Uh, guys," Lizzy said as they both looked at her. "Can you, like, stop arguing? It's not gonna help dad any."

Brunelle set his jaw, but didn't say anything. Kat hesitated, then exhaled loudly and took Lizzy's hand. "You're right, honey. I'm sorry. We're just trying to help your dad."

Brunelle nodded. 'Right. I'm sorry too." He rubbed the back of his neck. "And I don't really think he did it. That was just the lawyer in me talking. The regular person in me knows he's innocent."

Lizzy looked to each of the adults in turn and then lowered her eyes. "I wish _I_ knew that."

Kat squeezed her daughter's hand. "What do you mean, honey? Of course daddy's innocent."

Lizzy just shrugged.

"He is innocent, Lizzy" Brunelle insisted. "And the jury will see that. They'll find him not guilty."

Lizzy looked up at him. "How? You didn't get to ask the questions you wanted." She looked to her mom. "And you said he wasn't doing a very good job."

"He is doing a good job," Kat insisted. "I was just frustrated."

"Me too," Brunelle said. "Trials are stressful. I was just frustrated."

Kat looked down for a moment, then up at Brunelle. "I'm sorry. I shouldn't have told you not to ask any other questions. You're the lawyer."

Brunelle shook his head. "And you're the—" He was about to say 'wife' but stopped himself. Not because she was really the ex-wife. But because of what else she was. "You're the medical examiner." He smiled. "You're the fucking medical examiner."

Another F-bomb, but it seemed okay because he was smiling. Genuinely smiling.

Lizzy giggled at the word. Kat giggled too, but more of a nervous titter. "Yeah. And?"

Brunelle smiled broadly and raised his glass. "And you're going to testify."

CHAPTER 38

The next morning, the guards brought Jeremy to court, the bailiff led the jurors into the jury box, and the judge looked down at Brunelle.

"The defense may call its first witness."

Brunelle stood up, steeled for the battle he was about to incite.

"The defense calls Dr. Kat Anderson."

Kat stood up. But so did Westerly.

"Objection!" Westerly practically shouted as he jumped to his feet and slapped the table. It was the first time he'd lost his composure. He quickly regained it. "I believe," he said evenly, "we should discuss this outside the presence of the jury."

Brunelle could hardly disagree. He nodded to the judge. In turn, she nodded to her bailiff. In a few moments, he was closing the door to the jury room behind them. Once they were safely out of earshot, everyone but Westerly sat down.

"Your Honor," he began, with that calm confidence prosecutors have when they expect to win yet another motion or trial, "I was given no notice of this witness. In addition, she's a medical examiner, but I've been given no resume or expert reports to review. Furthermore, she's sat through the entire trial, in violation of the court's original—and standard—order that witnesses be excluded from the courtroom so they don't hear the testimony of other witnesses. Finally, Dr. Anderson is the ex-wife of the defendant, which, well, I'm not sure exactly how that impacts all this, but it must somehow. The People object to her being called as a witness, and move the court to exclude her testimony for the reasons I've just stated."

Brunelle expected to be asked why he'd violated the court order excluding witnesses and why he hadn't given notice to the prosecution and what he expected Kat to say.

Instead, Judge Carlisle looked past the lawyers to Kat. "Are you the defendant's ex-wife?"

Kat stepped forward. "Yes, Your Honor."

Carlisle nodded for a moment then tipped her head toward Lizzy. "Who's that?"

"Our daughter, Your Honor," Kat replied. "Elizabeth."

Lizzy nodded to the judge, then offered the slightest wave. Unprofessional, but endearing. Judge Carlisle narrowed her owlish eyes and glared at Brunelle.

"I expect Dr. Anderson will testify as to her opinions of Dr. Tuttle's autopsy," the judge half-asked.

"Yes, Your Honor," Brunelle confirmed.

"And you will disclose to the jury the personal interest she has in the outcome of the trial as the defendant's ex-wife and mother of his child?"

"Yes, Your Honor." Brunelle suppressed a smile at his growing hope that Kat would be allowed to testify.

Westerly suppressed his growing frustration. Carlisle looked to him. "Would you like an opportunity to interview the witness before she testifies?"

The question revealed her decision as to the underlying issue of whether Kat would be allowed to testify. The only issue left was whether they'd take a break while Westerly grilled Kat in the hallway.

But he was too experienced a prosecutor to need to do that. Or to keep fighting a battle he knew he'd lost. "No, Your Honor. Thank you, but I believe I know what the witness will testify to."

Carlisle allowed a small smile at Westerly's professionalism and the resultant lack of delay. She nodded to the bailiff who rose to bring in the jurors again. A few moments later Kat Anderson, M.D., was sworn in as the defense's first witness.

"Please state your name for the record," Brunelle began. This time he took the same spot Westerly had held for his direct exams — right next to the last juror in the jury box.

"Kat Anderson," she told the jurors. She knew to talk to them, not Brunelle.

"How are you employed, Miss Anderson?" Brunelle tried not to smile at the 'Miss Anderson.' He had to admit it was better than 'Miss. Anderson-Stephenson.' He ignored the other possible hyphenated-name. He needed to focus on the task at hand.

"I'm an assistant medical examiner with the King County Medical Examiner's Office in Seattle, Washington."

"So you're a medical doctor?"

Kat nodded. "Yes, you have to be an M.D. to work as a medical examiner."

Kat then listed off her degrees, residencies, and qualifications. At least as impressive as Dr. Tuttle. There was just one problem.

"Do you know the defendant?" Brunelle knew he had to ask.

The jurors likely expected an obligatory 'No' to confirm the witness' independence. Surprise.

"Yes," Kat looked over to Jeremy. "He's my ex-husband."

That sent a twitter through both the jury room and the gallery, including one reporter who jerked his head up, then dashed out into the hallway, undoubtedly to call an editor or something.

Brunelle had figured there were two ways to handle this little issue. Either have Kat explain her findings, win the jury over with her knowledge and charm, then mention the whole 'the defendant is my ex-husband' thing at the end, hoping the jury would overlook it after having decided she was credible on the merits. But he thought it was just as likely that they would throw out her entire testimony at that point, and feel tricked to boot. No, he decided; the better route was to admit the bias up front, then use that knowledge and charm of hers to win them over anyway.

"Do you have any children in common?" Just in case being married to him wasn't enough to destroy her credibility.

"Yes," Kat admitted. She smiled at Lizzy. "We have one daughter, Elizabeth. She's sitting in the front row."

Brunelle exhaled. Okay, that was done. And maybe for the better. Usually, the attorneys couldn't identify the friends and family who came to support the defendants or victims. It was left to the jury to speculate. Now they knew Jeremy had a real, flesh-and-blood daughter who loved him enough to come to court every single day. *Keep that in mind, ladies and gentlemen, as you consider your verdict.*

Now to the important stuff. "Did you have an opportunity," Brunelle asked, "to review the reports prepared by Dr. Sylvia Tuttle in this case?"

Kat returned her attention to the jurors. "Yes, I did. I was also present during a pretrial interview where she discussed her findings."

Brunelle had to smile. She was good. That interview was going to be important.

"And do you have an opinion as to the reliability of Dr. Tuttle's findings?"

Kat shrugged slightly. "I don't disagree with what she found. I disagree with the conclusions she drew from those findings. An autopsy is an autopsy. The physical evidence on and in the body doesn't change. But it has its limits. I don't believe Dr. Tuttle can reliably make the claims she testified to as to the exact manner in which Vanessa died."

Brunelle stole a glance at the jury. They seemed interested, if perhaps a bit dubious. Here was the ex-wife saying the county medical examiner was wrong. Not surprising. There were several pairs of crossed arms and at least one incredulous eyebrow. But they were interested too. Several were leaning forward, and all of them were looking at her.

"What specifically do you disagree with?" Brunelle asked.

Kat looked to the jurors. "Medical examiners deal in facts. We examine human remains—whether full bodies, parts of bodies, or skeletons—and try to determine what forces were applied to the body to cause injury and death. I was trained and strongly believe that the medical examiner's job stops at the examining room door. I can never tell you exactly what happened when a person died. I wasn't there. I can tell you a bullet went through the victim's lung, but I can't tell you who shot it or why. That's for the cops, not the docs,"

That was a nice touch. Brunelle noticed a few jurors smile at the cops/docs comment. *Good.* They liked her.

He took a moment to look at her, sitting on the witness stand, all confident and smart. He liked her too.

"So what was it in Dr. Tuttle's conclusions that went beyond what you might have been willing to conclude?"

Kat nodded then turned back to the jury. "I reviewed the reports, including all the photographs. There is no dispute that Vanessa's lungs were perfectly pink inside. From that, it is reasonable to conclude that she didn't inhale any smoke prior to her death. What's not reasonable is to speculate as to why that might be. Dr. Tuttle extrapolated from a medical observation to a conclusion better left to law enforcement."

"But if she was found inside a burned out building," Brunelle challenged, "but never breathed in any smoke, isn't it fair to conclude that she was dead before the fire started?"

"Maybe," Kat admitted with a shrug. "But maybe not. She was found in a back room, but the fire was mainly in the large dance area. There may be other reasons why she didn't breathe in the smoke. For example, fire and smoke rise. If she was on the floor…"

She stopped. Brunelle waited a beat, but she was lost in thought. After another moment, he had to prompt her. "If she was on the floor…?"

"If she was on the floor," Kat snapped out of her reverie, "she wouldn't have breathed in any smoke anyway. That's why they teach people to drop to the floor during a fire. There's no smoke down there."

Brunelle smiled slightly. He liked that. He was really going to like what she said next.

"In fact…" she started, but then stopped again, clearly trying to gather her thoughts. "Let me back up."

Then she turned fully in her seat toward the jurors. No more polite head turns. She was facing them directly. Class was in session.

"Every autopsy is different," she began. "People die from all sorts of things. Disease, car accidents, shootings. Some are easy to determine. If a body has five bullet holes through it, including one through the heart, I pretty much know he died from being shot. Diseases can be harder, depending on the disease. If there's a large cancerous tumor, I know where to look. But if there's nothing like that, then it can be hard to figure out what to look for. But the hardest thing is asphyxiation."

She looked at Brunelle for the next question. She wasn't supposed to just deliver a lecture. That would be objectionable as a narrative response, although a glance at Westerly showed him both interested and unlikely to interrupt.

"Uh, why is that?" Brunelle obliged.

Kat turned back to her students. "Asphyxiation is what happens when the body is deprived of oxygen, causing a condition called hypoxia which can lead to coma and death. The most common causes are strangulation and smothering."

"What's the difference?" Brunelle jumped in.

"Strangulation is constriction of the trachea that prevents sufficient air to the lungs," Kat explained. "Smothering occurs when a foreign object, like a pillow, blocks the nose and mouth and prevents air from entering the trachea in the first place,"

"Okay…" Brunelle wasn't sure what to ask next.

"But there's another way to asphyxiate," Kat prompted.

Good girl. "What's that?" he asked.

"Being in an oxygen-poor environment," Kat explained. "If there's not enough oxygen in the air, it doesn't matter how much you breathe, you'll asphyxiate."

Brunelle blinked at her. He managed not to tell her he loved her, but just barely.

"She was on the floor," he repeated.

"And fire burns up," Kat expounded. "When fire burns, its fuel is oxygen. It would have sucked all the air up and away from the floor where she was lying."

"So the reason her lungs were pink wasn't just that she didn't breathe in any smoke," Brunelle said, knocked out of his question-and-answer mode by Kat's realization.

"She didn't breathe any oxygen either," Kat finished.

A silence fell over the courtroom and Brunelle looked to the jury to see how they were taking Kat's testimony. The arms had all uncrossed and every one of them was leaning forward. He wanted to stop right then and there, but there was one small problem.

"What about the bruising on her throat?"

Oh yeah. That.

But Kat shook her head. "Those don't necessarily mean anything. They mean at some point prior to her death—when her heart was still pumping blood to make the bruises in the first place—

someone grabbed her throat. But asphyxiation doesn't leave visible injuries. In fact, there's a thing called 'burking.' It's named after a serial killer named Burke who killed his victims by getting them drunk, then sitting on their chests and covering their noses and mouths. The combination of compression of the lungs and lack of air caused asphyxiation, but there were no visible injuries and he would provide the bodies to medical schools."

Nice. Brunelle shook his head. *The things pathologists know.*

"But I thought strangulation victims suffered visible injuries to their eyes?" he asked. He actually knew how Kat would explain this, but the jury needed to hear it too, in case they'd seen too many episodes of C.S.I.

Kat nodded, in full doctor-professor mode. She turned to the jurors, who were eating it up. "I've testified about something called petechial hemorrhage," she said, "which is burst blood vessels in the eyes, very common in strangulation cases. But those are caused from the inability of the blood to leave the head during strangulation, not from the lack of oxygen to the lungs."

Brunelle nodded. "Was there any petechial hemorrhaging present here?" Brunelle asked.

"No," Kat shook her head with a slight smile. "Or Dr. Tuttle didn't bother looking for it. During her interview, she admitted she didn't even notice the bruising on the neck until after she'd cut open the chest and been surprised by the pink lungs. Later on, after the autopsy was complete, she examined the external photographs and noticed the bruises. But no, I didn't see any mention of petechial hemorrhaging anywhere in her reports."

Brunelle nodded. Everyone in the room had forgotten she was the defendant's ex-wife. She was just one hell of an M.E.

"Thank you, doctor. No further questions."

Brunelle walked over and sat down next to Jeremy, which immediately darkened his mood again. He loved interacting with Kat on any level. Being reminded she had an ex and a kid with him, not so much. Luckily, Westerly stood up and Brunelle could return his attention to the trial.

"Good morning, doctor," Westerly started.

"Good morning," Kat replied pleasantly enough.

Brunelle wondered how Westerly would play it. Option A was to smash on her obvious bias as the defendant's ex-wife; but that would ignore the weight of her medical testimony. Option B was to ignore that obvious bias—precisely because it was obvious—and cross her on her conclusions. Brunelle was hoping for Option A, so he was pretty sure Westerly would go with Option B.

"Thank you for coming here and testifying on behalf of your ex-husband," Westerly started. Perfect. A little jab to remind the jury, but it wasn't actually a question. And before Kat could jump in to respond to the insinuation, he posed an actual question she had to answer. "You didn't actually perform the autopsy in this case, did you?"

Kat shook her head. "No. I reviewed Dr. Tuttle's reports."

"And you didn't notice any errors or mistakes by her in performing that autopsy, did you?"

Kat twisted her mouth. "I think her external examination was perhaps inadequate if she didn't notice the bruising until after she opened up the body."

"You saw the photographs of the bruises, is that right?"

"Yes."

"And they were fairly light, weren't they?"

Kat thought for a moment, then agreed. "Yes. They were purple, indicating they hadn't had time to start healing before her death, but they weren't very dark at all."

Westerly nodded.

"And you agree that Ms. Stephenson didn't inhale any smoke prior to her death."

Kat thought about the question for a moment, then answered, "Yes, I would agree with that. At least not enough to darken the lung tissue."

"So really," Westerly said, "your objection to Dr. Tuttle's work isn't the autopsy, just the conclusions she drew from it."

Kat again thought for a moment, then again agreed. "I think that's fair. Her autopsy was adequate. But her conclusions were speculative."

Westerly nodded for several seconds, then gestured gently at her. "But again, you're the defendant's ex-wife?"

"I'm a doctor," Kat replied to the real question.

"And a mother," Westerly observed, He turned to look at Lizzy, and everyone else did too.

Kat frowned, but had to admit, "Yes."

"No further questions."

Carlisle looked to Brunelle. "Any re-direct examination?"

But Brunelle stood and shook his head slightly. Kat had done great. He could hardly hope to improve on it. "No, Your Honor. The witness may be excused."

Kat stepped down from the witness stand and retook her seat next to her daughter, who gave her a big hug.

Perfect, thought Brunelle. *Now to finish off the family photo.*

"The defense calls Jeremy Stephenson," he announced dramatically.

But Jeremy grabbed his sleeve and pulled him down to whisper frantically in his ear.

"No, I—" He glanced around at the courtroom full of expectant faces. "I have something I have to tell you."

CHAPTER 39

"What is it?" Brunelle demanded in his own brusque whisper.

But Jeremy shook his head and looked around the courtroom again. "I can't tell you here. Not in front of all these people."

Brunelle stood up straight to survey the room and ran a hand through his hair.

"Is there a problem, Mr. Brunelle?" Carlisle asked from her perch.

Brunelle frowned. "May I have a brief recess, Your Honor? I need to discuss a matter with my client."

This was exactly the kind of shit he didn't want to do in front of the jury. It made him look unorganized and his client look like he was hiding something. Whatever momentum they'd gotten from Kat's testimony was dissipating fast.

"How much time do you need?" Carlisle asked coldly.

Brunelle looked around again. The only thing close to private was the jury room, and that was going to be filled with twelve irritated jurors. "May I have a moment, Your Honor?"

Without waiting for an answer, he peered at the clock, then consulted quickly with the nearest corrections officer. "Your Honor," he said. "I know it's only ten thirty, but I'd ask that we adjourn until after lunch. I'll need to make some arrangements for a place to speak with my client."

Just in case any of the jurors weren't sure he was in custody. You don't need to 'make arrangements' to speak to someone who's allowed to walk into the hallway.

Carlisle sighed, then frowned, then sighed some more. But finally she acquiesced. "All right, Mr. Brunelle. We will be at recess until one o'clock. Be prepared to begin your examination at one o'clock sharp."

"Yes, Your Honor," Brunelle replied with a relieved sigh of his own. "Thank you."

"Court is at recess," Carlisle announced, and she retired to her chambers. The bailiff rose to excuse the jurors, and Brunelle stepped back to the corrections officer he'd spoken to. The officer nodded at Brunelle's suggestion and a few minutes later, the jurors had left the jury room and Brunelle and Jeremy stepped inside for a private conversation, the corrections officers guarding the exits.

"What is it?" Brunelle demanded. Jeremy had sat down at the conference table in the room. Brunelle was too agitated to sit. "This better be important. I don't think you realize how bad that looked."

Jeremy shrugged. "Oh, I do. But I think it could have looked a lot worse."

Brunelle ran a hand over his head again. "How?"

"There's something I didn't tell you," Jeremy admitted. "I think I better not testify."

"Are you fucking kidding me?" Brunelle snapped. "I just told the jury you were testifying. We talked about this. I can't tell them you're testifying and then not call you."

"You have to," Jeremy insisted.

"Why?"

"Because I lied to you," Jeremy said. "I wasn't home reading a book. I was at the studio."

Brunelle's arms dropped to his sides. He just stared at Jeremy for several seconds, absorbing the revelation. "Are you fucking kidding me?"

Jeremy shook his head. "No. I probably should have told you earlier."

"Probably?!" Brunelle yelled. "Probably? No. Definitely. You definitely should have told me. What the fuck, Jeremy? Do you not understand what's going on here? Do you not get what I'm trying to do? How the hell can I defend you if you lie to me? Jesus, you were there? What the hell am I supposed to do with that?"

Jeremy threw his hands wide. "Exactly. I figured if you thought I was at home, you could defend me better."

"Could?" Brunelle challenged, "or *would*? Damn it, Jeremy, I'm your attorney. I'll do my best no matter what. I don't care whether you did it or not."

Jeremy looked Brunelle in the eye. "Don't you?"

Brunelle was about to reply, but thought for a moment, and sighed. "Maybe I do care."

He sat down next to his client. "What happened, Jeremy? Tell me the truth. You have to tell me truth."

Jeremy nodded. "I will. I'm sorry. Here's what really happened."

Jeremy lowered his eyes and folded his hands on his lap. "We'd been having a lot of problems lately. The studio wasn't working out. It was really stressful. At first, I hadn't told her where I was getting the money from, but after a while I had to. We had to close the studio. It just wasn't going to work. But it just made her so mad. We hadn't been getting along anyway. We got into an argument at our place and she stormed out. She said she was going to the studio to make some calls. It was midnight, so I knew that was bullshit. But she left and I let her.

"After a while I started to get worried, though. I called and texted but she didn't answer. So I went over to the studio. She was in the back office on the phone with someone, but she hung up when I walked in. I demanded to know who it was, but she wouldn't tell me and we just started fighting again. It was crazy. She just wouldn't listen to me. I tried to grab her phone, but she punched me in the side of the head."

He smiled weakly at the memory. "It didn't hurt too bad, actually, but it surprised me. I grabbed her by the throat to get her under control. I admit, I was pissed, but then I saw the fear in her eyes and I realized I was out of control too. I pushed her away. She fell to the floor sobbing. I think she might have hit her head, I don't know. I was so angry, I just left."

He shrugged again. "The police came by later to tell me she was dead. That's why I asked if there were any witnesses. Because I'd grabbed her. But I didn't kill her. And I didn't set the fire." He looked up at Brunelle. "You have to believe me."

Brunelle chewed on his cheeks for a few seconds. "No, I don't," he replied. "I don't have to believe a damn word you say. Not after all the other lies you've told me."

He tapped his chin. "But I do believe you," he said. "Which means I can't put you on the stand. If you tell the jury that story, they'll convict you in two minutes, and only because one of them needed ninety seconds to pee."

"I could stick with the story about being at home reading a book," Jeremy suggested.

Brunelle shook his head. "No, I can't put you on the stand knowing you're lying. That's suborning perjury. I'd lose my license."

They both sat there for several moments. Finally, Jeremy asked, "So what are we going to do?"

Brunelle frowned, not because he didn't have any ideas. Suddenly, he did have one. He just wasn't sure it would work. Still, he couldn't think of anything else. And if it did work…

He took out his cell phone and called Sophia.

"Hello?" she answered in that amazing voice of hers.

"'Sophia. It's Brunelle. I need you drop everything and do me a favor. Listen carefully, and do exactly as I say..."

CHAPTER 40

One o'clock came and Brunelle was very much not ready. Carlisle took the bench anyway. The bailiff had already brought the jurors into the courtroom so they could start as soon as the judge came out.

"Mr. Stephenson," the judge addressed the defendant directly, "you may step forward to be sworn in."

"Uh, Your Honor," Brunelle stood to interrupt. "There's been a slight change in plan. I may need a few more minutes."

Carlisle raised an eyebrow. Brunelle wondered absently if real owls had eyebrows. "What sort of change in plans?"

"Uh..." Brunelle looked at the door to the hallway. It was frustratingly devoid of attractive private investigators. "Mr. Stephenson isn't going to testify after all."

The other owl eyebrow rose. "At all?"

Westerly's expression echoed the judge's question.

Brunelle threw another glance at the door. It had been a tall order to get everything done in just two and half hours, especially when Sophia had to come to the Hall of Justice first to get Brunelle's subpoena. But he had faith in her. He just needed to stall a bit more.

"How's that?" he asked.

Judge Carlisle frowned and leaned back in her leather high-backed chair. "I said, is your client not testifying at all, or are you just changing the order of your witnesses?"

"Um," Brunelle replied with another glance at the very not opening hallway door. "I'm not entirely certain about that, Your Honor." It was okay if he lied to the court, he thought sardonically, he just couldn't call a witness to do it. "But he's definitely not testifying next."

Carlisle's frown deepened and the owl-brows lowered. "Then who is your next witness, Mr. Brunelle?"

At that point the door to the hallway finally swung open and in walked Sophia Farinelli. Her hair was jet black, falling to her chest in soft waves, with a red blouse and thick silver bracelets. Definitely Wonder Woman.

Brunelle raised his own questioning eyebrow at his investigator. Sophia smiled and nodded. Then Brunelle turned back to the judge. "The defense calls Laura Mayer."

Sophia peered into the hallway and gestured to the waiting Laura Mayer. She walked in reluctantly, a frown on her face, both her hands clutching her purse in front of her like some sort of shield. She couldn't have looked less comfortable.

Sophia pointed to the witness stand and whispered something in her ear. Laura nodded and she walked past Brunelle without looking at him. The judge swore her in and she sat down on the witness stand, the purse still clutched on her lap.

Rather than walk over to his spot next to the jury box, or even his place at the bar, Brunelle opted to pose his questions from where he stood at counsel table, right next to his client. It was usually the lazy or unprofessional attorneys who asked their questions from their table—the worst offenders not even bothering to stand up. But Brunelle wasn't being lazy or unprofessional. He didn't want Laura looking to the jury when she answered his questions. He wanted her to look at Jeremy.

"Good afternoon," he began.

Laura surrendered a tight nod. "Hello."

"Could you please state your name for the record?"

"Laura Mayer."

Normally, Brunelle might next have asked if she knew the defendant. It was a standard, non-leading way to explain to the jury how the witness was related to the case. But this wasn't the normal case, and he wasn't calling her for the normal reasons. So instead, he asked, "Did you know the victim, Vanessa Stephenson?"

Even the question was a dangerous concession. Whether Vanessa was actually a 'victim' was the whole point of the trial; the jury would decide that. Then again, Vanessa was dead, so maybe the issue wasn't whether she was a victim, but rather what she was a victim of.

"Yes," was Laura's simple response. She was still clutching her purse, tense as a snare drum.

"How did you know her?"

Laura thought for a moment before answering, "She was my business partner. And a friend."

Brunelle nodded. That's what he wanted her to say. The jury needed to hear those things. Both of those things.

"What was your business?"

"We were co-owners of a dance studio in the SOMA district," Laura answered. "Inner Beauty Dance and Dreams."

Brunelle stole a glance at the jury to see what they thought of the name. It was idealistic, almost silly. But then again, it was San Francisco. The jurors seemed to appreciate the name.

"And how did you come to open that studio with Vanessa?"

Laura nodded, then relaxed a bit as she surrendered herself to memories more comfortable than her present circumstances. "Well, we met at an arts exhibition downtown. It was a fund raiser for youth art programs. She was very devoted to the arts. So am I. We began discussing the arts community here in San Francisco. We got on quite well and agreed to meet up again sometime for coffee. Eventually she mentioned her dream of opening a dance studio and I mentioned my desire to use my resources to expand the reach of the arts. I guess you could say the idea was both of ours."

That was a nice story. Laura was a nice lady. So was Vanessa, Brunelle was sure. It was important the jury see the genuine affection Laura had for Vanessa. It would explain a lot.

"How did the business fare?" Brunelle pushed into less comfortable territory.

Laura's expression reflected the change. It went from wistful to pained. "Not very well, I'm afraid."

"Why is that?"

Laura shrugged "It lost money right out of the gate, and just kept losing more. We knew it would take a while to turn around, but we didn't realize how bad it would be. Vanessa..." Laura shook her head, but fondly. "Vanessa just couldn't say no. She took on students who couldn't pay, so we hired instructors we couldn't pay, and bought equipment we couldn't afford. It just got worse and worse."

Brunelle nodded in a way that he hoped looked sympathetic. "Is that typical with artistic ventures?" He guessed it might be.

"Not always," Laura replied, "but it's not uncommon. A business needs to be run as a business. If it's run as a hobby, it's likely doomed."

"Is that what this was?" Brunelle asked. "Vanessa's hobby?"

Laura gave a quick shake of her head. "No. It was her dream."

"But you can't pay the bills with a dream, can you?" Brunelle echoed Westerly's opening remarks.

"No," Laura agreed. "But Vanessa was very passionate about the studio. Almost too much so. She didn't want to be bothered with the financial side of it. But that sort of thing can't be ignored indefinitely."

"So who bankrolled Vanessa's dream?"

This was the beginning of the pay off, the reason he'd rushed Sophia out the door with a hastily drafted subpoena for Laura Mayer. But he wasn't quite there yet.

"At first," Laura said, a bit proudly, "I did. But I could only do so much."

"And when you were tapped out, who stepped in?"

Laura finally looked at Brunelle's client. The defendant. The accused murderer of her friend. She nodded at him. "Jeremy."

So the victim's friend and supporter just told the jury that Jeremy was actually a loving husband who supported his wife's untenable dream of owning a dance studio. Brunelle smiled inside and mentally checked off the first of his two goals for Laura's direct exam. He didn't know if he'd get the second goal.

"What did Jeremy do to prop it up?"

"He loaned money to the studio," Laura answered after a moment's hesitation. It was always artificial when an attorney and witness went through the dance of question-and-answer about information they both already knew. But Brunelle and Laura were walking into an even more uncomfortable area: questions and answers about information they both already knew, and knew was supposed to be secret.

But trials were truth-seeking exercises.

"Loaned?" Brunelle questioned.

Laura gave a begrudging nod. "Gave," she corrected. "He gave money to the studio."

"And did that succeed in getting the studio onto sound financial footing?" Brunelle knew the answer was no, but he thought he finally understood why. And what it meant.

"No," Laura shook her head. "Not really."

Brunelle was about to head onto dangerous ground. Well,

maybe not dangerous, but unknown. He didn't know how much Laura would give him, and it occurred to him there was someone else who might get in his way: Westerly. But a quick glance at his opponent showed him to be interested, apparently earnest in his desire to hear what Laura had to say, and nowhere near objecting. Brunelle relaxed a bit. But only a bit.

"Why not?"

Brunelle had watched lots of police interrogations. One thing detectives often told the suspects was something along the lines of, 'When I ask a question, I already know the answer. I'm just checking to see if you'll tell me the truth.' Half the time, it was bullshit, but it usually worked.

He knew the answer to his question. He wondered if Laura would tell him the truth.

She shifted in her seat and clutched her purse tighter. She looked at Brunelle, then Jeremy, then down. She didn't look at the jury.

"I had lost a lot of money," she said quietly. "I knew Jeremy's money would only delay the inevitable, not prevent it. I decided to withdraw my investment from the business while I still could."

Good, thought Brunelle. She'd told the truth. Even if she'd hidden it inside big words.

"You took Jeremy's money out without telling anyone," he translated, "to get back the money you'd lost?"

Laura nodded slowly and sighed. "Yes."

It was interesting, and interesting was always good for a trial attorney. But it wasn't quite enough.

"But Vanessa wouldn't shut the studio down, would she?"

Laura shook her head. "No. It was her passion. Her dream. Nothing was going to deter her. Not even the financial realities." She chuckled mirthlessly. "Least of all the financial realities. It wasn't about money. It was about art."

This was the tricky part. That second goal on his checklist. He could walk her up to it, slowly, so the jury could understand it. Or he could take advantage of the intimacy that shared knowledge gives two people. He knew. She knew he knew. And she was ready to tell the truth.

"Jeremy took out a dangerous loan from some loan sharks to make up his losses," he said, more statement than question. "And you agreed to pay back that loan for him from the insurance money you got from the fire."

Laura looked over to Jeremy again and admitted, "Yes."

Brunelle looked at him too, then back to his witness. He ignored Westerly's stunned expression. "And you never would have loaned money to someone you knew had murdered your friend Vanessa, would you?'

Laura looked down again and shook her head, "No."

Pay off time.

"You didn't answer the phone when Vanessa called you that night because you didn't want her to know you weren't home, right?"

Laura just nodded. Technically, he should have asked her to respond out loud for the court reporter. But this wasn't for the court reporter; it was for the jury.

"You didn't know she was in the back room when you set the fire, did you?"

A hush fell over the courtroom as Laura Mayer sat in the witness chair, her hands still on her purse, but no longer clutching it. The truth did set you free. And it could set others free too.

"No," she said quietly without looking up. "I had no idea. She wasn't supposed to be there. It was one in the morning. No one was supposed to be there." Her lips started to tremble and she looked up at Brunelle. "Something had to give. It wasn't working. But she wouldn't listen. I thought... I thought if the studio had a fire, well, then she'd have to walk away. We would split the insurance money and part as friends."

"But instead," Brunelle observed, "you just parted."

Laura nodded. Tears were welling in her eyes. "I am sorry. I never meant for anyone to get hurt. I don't know why she was there. She shouldn't have been there."

Brunelle nodded. "I know."

The hush hadn't abated. If anything it had deepened.

Brunelle looked up at the judge. "No further questions."

Carlisle watched him walk back to his seat and sit down next to Jeremy, who was bursting to say something, but didn't dare break the silence that had settled over the courtroom. Then the judge looked to Westerly. "Mr. Westerly?"

She didn't ask if he had any questions. Westerly knew what she was really asking. He nodded and stood up.

"Your Honor," he said, "the people move to dismiss the charges against Mr. Stephenson."

Judge Carlisle nodded. "Motion granted. Case dismissed."

EPILOGUE

The flight back to Seattle was more than relaxing. Normally Brunelle wasn't a fan of cramped seats, too-small snacks, and expensive drinks, but the case was over, he was on his way home, and Kat was beside him.

Yamata had been wrong. The post-trial celebrations did involve hugging, but Jeremy hugged Lizzy while Kat's hugs were exclusively Brunelle's. They had celebrated his victory that night as well. Three times.

There was just one thing that kept bugging Kat.

"Come on, David," she tried again as the plane neared the Seattle airport. "What did Jeremy tell you in the jury room? I promise I won't tell."

But Brunelle shook his head. "I really can't, Kat. It's attorney-client privilege. If he reported me to the bar, I could be suspended, or worse."

"He doesn't have to know," Kat responded.

Brunelle grinned but shook his head again. "No, you'd let it slip. Believe me. You think you wouldn't, but I know what it is, and some time when you're talking to him about something, you'd forget you're not supposed to know and say something about it. Trust me, it's better if you don't know."

In more ways than one, he thought.

"Hmph," Kat pouted. Then she wrapped her arm through his and laid her head on his shoulder. "I think you kind of liked being a defense attorney. It gave you a chance to be the bad boy."

Brunelle leaned over and kissed the top of her head. He really liked kissing the top of her head. "Do you like bad boys?"

Kat pulled her head from his shoulder and looked him in the eyes. "Maybe. Do you like bad girls?"

Brunelle just smiled and leaned in to kiss her—when Lizzy popped her head over from the seat behind.

"Would you two stop being so fucking adorable?"

Both of the adults just stared at her for a moment, then Kat burst out laughing and Brunelle lowered his head into his hand, smiling.

"Sit down, young lady," Kat finally managed to say through her giggles. "This is none of your business."

"None of your fucking business," Brunelle corrected, looking up again.

Kat nodded, trying to seem serious. "Right. What he said."

Lizzy smiled and blew a kiss at her mom, then plopped back down in her seat again.

"Thank you for making it okay for my daughter to say that word," Kat jokingly snarled. "You do like being the bad boy."

Brunelle grinned and gave her a quick, hard kiss. "You can punish me when we get home."

END

THE DAVID BRUNELLE LEGAL THRILLERS
Presumption of Innocence
Tribal Court
By Reason of Insanity
A Prosecutor for the Defense
Substantial Risk
Corpus Delicti
Accomplice Liability
A Lack of Motive
Missing Witness
Diminished Capacity
Devil's Plea Bargain
Homicide in Berlin
Premeditated Intent
Alibi Defense
Defense of Others
Necessity

THE TALON WINTER LEGAL THRILLERS
Winter's Law
Winter's Chance
Winter's Reason
Winter's Justice
Winter's Duty
Winter's Passion

THE RAIN CITY LEGAL THRILLERS
Burden of Proof
Trial by Jury
The Survival Rule

.

ABOUT THE AUTHOR

Stephen Penner is an author, artist, and attorney from Seattle, Washington. He has written over 30 novels and specializes in courtroom thrillers known for their unexpected twists and candid portrayal of the justice system. He draws on his extensive experience as a criminal trial attorney to infuse his writing with realism and insight.

Stephen is the author of several top-rated legal thriller series. *The David Brunelle Legal Thrillers* feature Seattle homicide D.A. David Brunelle and a recurring cast of cops, defense attorneys, and forensic experts. *The Talon Winter Legal Thrillers* star tough-as-nails Tacoma criminal defense attorney Talon Winter. And *The Rain City Legal Thrillers* deliver the adventures of attorney Daniel Raine and his unlikely partner, real estate agent/private investigator Rebecca Sommers.

For more information, please visit *www.stephenpenner.com*.

Made in the USA
Monee, IL
17 November 2024